Inherent Legacy

By

Aaron Achartz

[signature]

authorHOUSE

1663 Liberty Drive, Suite 200
Bloomington, Indiana 47403
(800) 839-8640
www.AuthorHouse.com

This book is a work of fiction. Places, events, and situations in this story are purely fictional and any resemblance to actual persons, living or dead, is coincidental.

© 2004 Aaron Achartz.
All Rights Reserved.

No part of this book may be reproduced, stored in a retrieval system, or transmitted by any means without the written permission of the author.

First published by AuthorHouse 07/27/04

ISBN: 1-4184-8891-7 (e)
ISBN: 1-4184-8892-5 (sc)

Library of Congress Control Number: 2004095843

Printed in the United States of America
Bloomington, Indiana

This book is printed on acid-free paper.

Dedicated to my parents, Julie Mohlis and Thomas Achartz, for their help, love, and support – A.A.

Prologue

"What could've I said?"

"Watch out for the meniscus, perhaps?"

Jim Owen leaned back in his lawn chair, and enjoyed his favorite spring past time, watching his friends, Sara Young and Greg Fields argue.

A flock of geese flew overhead, while a pile of unmelted snow was still at the end of the cul-de-sac. Jim had a t-shirt on, but evening still came quickly in early April, bringing with it cooler temperatures.

He was sitting across the patio table on a deck outside of Greg's house. The shrubs along the fence that ran the perimeter of the yard were just beginning to bloom as Greg and Sara's shouting echoed through the peaceful neighborhood.

They were always arguing about something. It might be politics, school, homework, an obscure surgery method, but they were always fighting.

Today was no different. They began to argue on whether cloning was ethical. They had done a cloning experiment in school, but it had not gone quite as expected.

"You should have not been so clumsy," Greg said.

"I wasn't clumsy," Sara retorted. "You hit me."

"You shouldn't have been cloning any living being anyway."

"Why not?"

Greg was always using his technical expertise to get Sara, but she had strong beliefs to back up her beliefs.

"It is not ethical," Greg said, "because it is creating another living thing, and taking life itself in to our hands."

"What if it could save a person's life?" Sara retaliated.

"By taking another's?" Greg said, pushing Sara.

"So, you have nothing intelligent to say, so you push me?"

"Guys!" Jim shouted. "Stop fighting, we are supposed to be working on our science project."

"We were, until Ms. Smarty-pants here had to say it was unethical. Or ethical, or something that was wrong," Greg said, sitting down at the patio table.

"I believe it was Greg who started this," Sara said, also sitting down.

Jim rolled his eyes. "I don't care, just stop arguing."

Greg and Sara sneered at each other and sat down at the round table on the deck. After a few seconds, though, they seemed to forget that they had fought at all

Jim knew, however, that this would only stop them for a few minutes. They soon would come upon another subject they agree upon. Then they would begin to fight anew.

He quickly started to lay out the materials for their project. Their poster was almost finished, they only had to glue on the facts and photos. Jim put all the supplies in a small pile.

"Okay, all we have left is to paste all of the writing and pictures on to here," Jim said, flattening a large piece of paper.

"I can do that," Sara said. She reached across, but her arm hit a glass of lemonade. Jim was able to grab all the work for the project, but Greg's papers were soaked.

"Only you could have done this!" Greg shouted as he stood up.

"Me?" Sara asked, also getting to her feet. "If you hadn't had the papers so far away."

"You are saying it is my fault?"

"I will glue the papers on for us, see you guys at school tomorrow," Jim said, but neither heard him.

He walked out the white gate in the front yard. Behind him, he could hear Greg and Sara still arguing. Eventually they would figure out he was gone.

Jim stuffed the supplies in to his backpack, slung it over his shoulder, and wheeled his bike away from the garage.

Why is life so monotonous? He thought as he biked down the road toward the library. He could finish the project there in peace.

PART 1

April 8, 2004

Chapter 1

The din of the two-hundred and fifty other students reverberated around the lunchroom. Jim walked from the lunch line, carrying his plate full of spaghetti with meatballs.

He sat down at the usual table, across from Greg. He opened his milk, and took a sip, then set it back down.

"There," he said, pointing to the corner of the lunchroom. Stuck on the ceiling was a small box. It had black and red wires going in between the cracks in the tiles and a small glass window facing them.

"Jim, are you still going on about those stupid cameras?" Greg asked, spinning his spaghetti around his fork. He lifted the fork carefully, making sure not to drop any sauce on his khakis and pressed white shirt.

"Yes, as a matter of fact I am," Jim said. He lifted his spaghetti to eat it, and a small red drop fell on his new blue jeans. He grabbed a napkin quickly, and wiped it off. He finished the bite, careful not to drop any on his red t-shirt.

"Hey guys," Sara said, tossing her tray on to the table. She slid in, and quickly began to eat her food.

"So," Sara said through a mouthful of food, "what are we talking about today?"

"Jim's still going on about the cameras," Greg said, rolling his eyes, and then taking a drink of milk.

"The video cameras?" Sara asked. "They're kind of interesting, but I think you are making a big deal out of it."

Greg groaned from across the table, and Jim looked at him, "What?"

"You always obsess over the smallest things," Greg said. "First it was Mr. Harcourt. Then it was who was right about the cafeteria food, you or Sara. Now it's the video cameras the school has in the rooms."

"Come on, I am serious," Jim slammed his milk to emphasize, but instead the milk squirted out the top, and oozed all over his hand.

Sara began to laugh hysterically. She was barely able to say, "We believe you Jim," before she burst out laughing more.

Tears were streaming down her face, and she was shaking. She just started to calm down, when she fell backward off the back of the bench. This caused her to laugh even harder and louder, and most of the lunchroom looked to see what was going on.

"Okay, that's it," Greg said, taking his empty tray and standing up. His eyebrows were furrowed, and he was glaring at Sara.

"I'll be back when you two can control yourselves," he said, and walked toward the front of the lunchroom. He dropped his dishes off at the dish drop.

After he dropped his dishes off, he began to walk around the lunchroom. Jim sighed. Greg did this every time Sara was goofing off. He would get up and walk once or twice around the room.

Jim watched him the whole time, while Sara was pulling herself off the floor, and putting her red Twins cap back on. She finished her lunch, and pushed the tray aside as Greg came back. When Sara saw Greg, she tried hard not to break out laughing again.

"I don't know," Greg said, sitting down again, "how you ever got in to a school for gifted students. All you ever seem to do is goof of and play games all day. You even make jokes about the schoolwork.

"It is an honor and a privilege to be part of this school and you should..."

"Always have the utmost respect for the teachers and the learning material," Sara finished for him. "You know, Greg, you really ought to get a new speech. I hear the same one everyday, and I can honestly say it's starting to get boring after three years."

"She's right," Jim said, finishing his milk, and pushing his tray aside. "You need to lighten up and enjoy life more. Most people don't enjoy being around someone who can not have a good time."

"I can have a good time," Greg said. "I am just as much fun as you and Sara. I enjoy trivia games, working on homework, and uh..."

"Can't think of anything else, can you?" Sara asked, smirking at him.

"I can too," Greg snapped, "just wait a second while I think of where I should start."

"Is there any place to start on an existentless list?" Sara asked.

"There is a list, and the word is un-existent!" Greg yelled, but calmed down when a few other kids turned to look at him. "You just tease me because you are jealous."

"Jealous? Not in a million years," said Sara. She pointed her finger at him. "You are the one who is jealous of me."

"I'm not!" Greg shouted back.

"Guys!" Jim yelled, putting his arm in-between them. "Stop this bickering. Now, let's get back to the cameras."

"You're still going on about the stupid cameras?" Greg asked and then rolled his eyes.

"Yes, I am. I think it is a mystery that needs to be solved," Jim said. "I just need to figure out where the security room is."

"I think I know," Greg said, unzipping his binder, and searching quickly through the organized folders.

"What is he looking for now?" Sara asked. Jim just shrugged his shoulders.

"Ah, here it is," Greg said, pulling out a normal white sheet of paper.

"What's that," Sara asked, reaching for it.

"Don't touch," Greg said, studying the sheet closely with a magnifying glass. "This is a map that was given to me on the first day of school by Ms. Harcourt."

"She gave you a map?" Jim asked, standing up, and leaning over the map. It was a very cryptic blueprint plan. He could barely tell what a hallway was, and what a pipe was.

"You won't be able to get in there easily," Sara said, pointing out a line in the midst of other lines. She outlined a rectangular area. "You'll have to get past Ms. Cleveland, the Principal's secretary."

"There's got to be another way in," Jim said looking at the map. "Are there any windows?"

"Just this one," Greg said, pointing. "But it's only twenty-four by eighteen inches."

"Way too small, Jim said, looking around the perimeter of the room. "What's that?"

"That looks like a vent, according to the key," Greg said. "These dimensions look like you could get in to the room easily. Now you just need a way to get in to the vent system."

"Cool!" Sara said. "We can climb through the air ducts, just like the spies in the movies!"

She did a squeal, and a small jump. Several other students looked at her, but then went back to what they were doing.

"Keep it down," Jim whispered.

"Sorry," Sara said, sitting back down. "So, are we going to go find a vent to climb through?"

"They stood up, and Sara and Jim dropped there dishes at the dish drop. They walked up to the door, and signed the sheet saying they were going to take some free time out side.

"Let's go," Sara said, skipping down the hall. Jim and Greg quickly followed. They stopped right behind Sara.

"What is it?" Greg asked, seeing Sara pointing at something.

"The vents look at them," Sara said. Jim leaned around her and looked. The vent was about a foot square.

"Well, we can cancel those plans, and go on with our normal lives," Greg said, turning and walking back toward the lunchroom.

"Wait," Jim said, "we should try to look outside before we give up. The vents may be larger out there."

Greg groaned, but turned around and followed them out the front door. The sunshine was extremely bright and warm compared to the mechanical feeling of the fluorescent lights.

It was the middle of April, but it felt like the Fourth of July. The air was hot, but the humidity was low. The sky was clear from one horizon to the other.

Several students were playing an impromptu soccer game on the soccer field far to the left. Ahead a long asphalt path stretched toward an open metal gate in a tall brick wall.

To Jim's right the flower garden was a dead brown and drying up in the early summer. A small drought was putting a lot of pressure on the gardening class to keep as many of the flowers alive as they could.

Walking under a tall pine, which the turn around went around, Jim turned to look up at the three story building. It looked small from the front, but it stretched back, twisted and turning where several additions had been added o.

Perched on top, above the main entrance, bright metal letters glistened in the sun. From all around the large plot of land they owned, you could always read it. *Bernel's School for Gifted Students: Where the Intellectual and Experimental Combine.*

Jim walked around the corner, with Greg and Sara trailing behind. The property sloped down and in to deep woods. Beyond the woods was the gorgeous Lake Minnetonka.

A lone sailboat skimmed across the waves. It was headed toward Excelsior, skipping across small waves created by the small breeze.

"Oh, I wish I was in that sailboat right now," Jim said, leaning against the school.

"Yeah," Sara agreed. "Wouldn't it be so fun to just fly across the waves?"

"You guys, over here," Greg called. Jim had not even noticed Greg had disappeared behind a dying bush. He was kneeling in front of a large metal grate. It would be easy to crawl through there.

"So, I think it will work better than I thought it would," Jim said, looking at Sara. "Do you think it will work?"

"Yeah, definitely," she said, kneeling down to look at it. "It's a good thing I suggested we look outside."

"No, I suggested we look outside," Jim said.

"Excuse me," Greg said, standing up, "but I will not let either of you take credit for my idea."

"Your idea?" Jim and Sara shouted together.

"It was definitely mine," Sara said, crossing her arms defiantly.

"No it was MINE," Greg said, leaning over her.

Jim turned away and sat down on a dying piece of grass. He took out a scrap piece of paper and began to sketch out a plan. Too soon, the bell rang, and it was time to change classes.

Students at the school could choose what classes to spend their time in, as long as they met the minimum requirements for each week. Jim always did the required classes at the beginning of the week, so he was free to go where he wanted.

"I'm going to free-writing area, like I do every Thursday, to plan" Jim said, "Are you coming with?"

"You bet!" Sara said, jumping and following Jim toward the door.

"You guys can do what you want, I am through," Greg said, turning and walking toward the art area.

"Oh, come on Greg," Sara said, grabbing his arm.

"Let go!" Greg said, pushing Sara's hand off his arm. "Fine, I will go along. However, you two must plan it with out me."

"Okay, whatever," Sara said, turning and going inside. "Come on, Jim let's go to the gym instead."

"Great idea, Sara. We can exercise and think," Jim said sarcastically. Then he called after Greg, "Hey, Greg!"

"Yeah?" Greg said, turning around.

"I will e-mail you with the specifics after school. Hopefully, we'll go tonight."

"I can't wait."

Chapter 2

The hollow thuds of dribbling basketballs echoed through the large gym. On one side of the court most of the class was playing a game of lightning. On the other side, Jim and Sara were playing one-on-one.

Jim glanced at the double doors to his left. He didn't see Sara pass as she jumped and shot, scoring another point.

"Are you looking to run away?" Sara asked, grabbing the basketball, and passing it to Jim.

"No way," Jim said, dribbling to the centerline, swiveling, and scoring a basket. "Yeah, in your face!"

Inherent Legacy

Sara grabbed the ball after the first bounce, and dribbled back to the center. She stopped on the opposite side of the line, just dribbling.

"Well, come on," Jim said.

"Just giving you time to get your energy back. I want to make things a little fairer for you," Sara said.

"You're the one who should be worried," Jim said, but Sara pushed right past him. He caught up, and hit the basketball before it could land in the basket.

"You know," Jim said, looking at the double doors leading in to the hall, "I think it's a fire hazard having only one route of escape."

"What are you talking about Sara said, mindlessly dribbling the ball.

"Those doors," Jim said as he pointed at them.

"There are other doors," Sara said.

"Yeah, but they are mostly rusted shut," Jim said, grabbing the basketball, and dribbling to center court. He took a three-point shot, but it bounced off the rim. Jumping up he grabbed the ball, and made a slam-dunk.

"So," Sara said, "how are we going to get to the school tonight?"

"Well, you do know there is a dock down by the lake?"

"There is?" Sara asked. Her basketball hit the backboard and flew to the side.

"Yeah, I think next year they are going to offer a canoeing class," Jim said, and then he ran over to retrieve the basketball.

"Your not as good as you claim," Jim said, passing it to her.

"So how does the dock help us?" Sara asked. She shot again, and this time it went in perfectly.

"Except for the lake side, there are walls around the perimeter of the property. I think that would be the easiest way to get on to the grounds."

Jim took his shot and it landed in the basket with as much precision as Sara's.

"Is that a challenge?" Sara said, grabbing the ball, and dribbling it menacingly.

"No, I do not want to challenge you," Jim said, turning away.

"Oh, come on wimp," Sara taunted.

"I am not a wimp," Jim said, turning around and grabbing the ball. He dribbled to center court, and faced away from the hoop.

He dribbled it a few times and stood still. He threw it straight back over his head, and it landed perfectly in the middle of the basket.

"Do better than that," Jim said, turning and walking away.

"You cheated somehow," Sara shouted after him, but Jim was not listening.

"Where are you going?" Sara called.

"I am going to tell Greg about the plans," Jim said, trying to open one of the large metal doors. "I decided not to e-mail him, just to tell him in person."

Sara dribbled to center court. She stopped and watched him struggle with opening the door.

"You would not be able to open that door if you had a rocket launcher!" Sara taunted, but it had no effect on Jim. He was able to jerk open the door, and walk away up the sloped hallway beyond.

"Why that little," Sara started, but stopped. She pounded the basketball in to the ground then turned to watch the rest of the class playing lightning.

"I do not care about him. He would have lost anyway," Sara said. She walked toward the rest of the class, throwing the ball over her shoulder.

She did not even noticed when the ball landed in the basket, and bounced away from the hoop. It bounced lower each bounce until it was rolling.

Then it rolled until it came to rest against a large box covered with a sheet. In dark black letters on the bottom of the box read *Keep in a sealed and inspected containment chamber only!*

Chapter 3

Jim slowly opened the door to the art class, and peeked in. Mr. Stevens, the art teacher, was starting a new lesson on how to paint by using the Turner watercolor technique.

Mr. Stevens was the art and woods teacher, but he should have taught just woods. He did not appreciate all of the different styles of art, he just enjoyed art that looked like finger-paint.

The classroom had counters with several sinks running around the edge, with one end open on to a balcony. A cool breeze blew in off the lake.

Jim slipped in to the classroom and went over to an empty easel next to Greg's easel. He took out his paints and began drawing a lake.

The picture windows behind Mr. Stevens provided Jim with a perfect view of Lake Minnetonka and Excelsior beyond. He painted for several minutes with long, curved brush strokes.

"So," Greg said, finally leaning over, "why did you come here?"

"I felt like painting," Jim said, and went back to working on his painting.

"What is the plan for our infiltration?" Greg asked, not paying attention to his painting. Jim's painting was going great, and seemed to have captured the essence of Lake Minnetonka. Greg's was many blobs on paper.

"The plan is to meet at my house tonight to finish working on our science project."

"I thought we had already – oh, I get it," Greg said, his hand again aimlessly moving around the canvas.

Jim finished and put his paints in to his bag. He zipped it up, and grabbed a piece of paper off the counter. The paper was a rubric Jim used to start critiquing his work. Mr. Stevens looked over toward them and started walking toward them.

"Amazing," he said, approaching as if he was going to hug the canvas. "This is the most inspired, beautiful piece I have seen yet."

He walked right past Jim and was gesturing at Greg's painting. "Look how the lines accent the feeling behind the power of the lake."

Greg ducked away and went over to Jim, catching him before he left, "What do you see?"

"Where," Jim asked, looking around for something special.

"In my 'masterpiece'," Greg said.

"A bunch of blobs," Jim admitted. "I really do not see any point to your painting."

"Yeah, blobs," Greg said. "That's all I saw."

Chapter 4

Jim looked out the window, pushing the curtain to the side.

"Jim," his mother said, "don't do that, you'll wreck the curtain."

"Jeez mom, I won't wreck it," he said, and went back to looking out the window. The first person to arrive was Greg. His dad pulled his blue sedan in to the driveway, and pushed Greg out the door.

"Be home by eleven, or else I am warning you!" His dad yelled at him, then reversed the car and drove erratically away.

"Greg, are you okay?" Jim asked, opening the door and running out on to the porch.

"Yeah, but this was one of the nights my father wanted to be with me," Greg said as they walked inside. He threw his backpack on to the floor next to the door. "I do not know why, but I hate spending time with him, even though it is only two nights a month."

"Are you sure you are okay?" Jim asked, picking up Greg's backpack and walking to his room. "Why don't you tell your mom?"

"No, I can't do that," Greg said.

"Why not?" asked Jim.

"My dad, he doesn't get to spend much time with me, so he gets mad when I don't spend all my time with him during his free time."

"Can't you do anything by yourself?" Jim asked.

Before Greg could answer, the doorbell rung.

"Well, you can't?" Jim asked. Greg just shrugged his shoulders a little and looked at his feet.

A few seconds later the doorbell rung again. Jim shrugged his shoulders and ran to the door. He opened it right before Sara rung the door a third time.

"One ring is enough, you know," Jim said, opening the door for Sara.

"Hello to you too, happy," Sara said, hanging her jacket on a hook. "It sure gets chilly at night doesn't it?"

"Yeah," Jim said. "Greg and I were just talking about-"

"Forget about it Jim," Greg said. "I am fine."

Jim looked at his reaction trying to judge what his real feelings were. He finally said," Okay, let's get working on our project."

"What's left," Greg asked. "I thought we were done?"

"Wait, I thought we were going to go to the school," Sara whispered as they walked in to Jim's room.

"We are, but our project is due tomorrow," Jim reminded her.

"Tomorrow's Thursday already?" Sara asked.

"Yes, it is Thursday," Greg said, looking at his watch. "So, Jim, what do we have left?"

"Just have to glue these three things on," Jim said, handing both Greg and Sara a small pack of papers. Each was about the size of a note card.

Jim had only two cards and glued them on quickly. He got up, and slowly peeked out his bedroom door. He could see down the hall and toward the kitchen and living room.

A counter separated the two, with Jim's mother working behind it. She was filling out some paper work. Occasionally she would look up and out the picture windows at Lake Minnetonka.

His mother set down her papers, and seemed to remember a chore she had forgotten. Walking over toward the door to the basement, she flipped a light switch. A few seconds later, the door was closed.

Seeing the coast was clear, Jim ran low to the floor and grabbed a set of keys off the counter. He slipped on the slick wood floors and almost fell. The keys were slightly smaller than normal keys, and the key chain was a red speedboat.

He could hear his mother in the basement, locking up the patio door. One side of the basement was in the hill, but the other side was open to Lake Minnetonka.

Quickly sprinting back to his room, Jim tried to be quiet. His mother was climbing back up the basement stairs. He slid in the door and shut it moments before his mom opened the door from the basement.

"I got them," he said, breathing heavy, but dangling the keys. "We'll leave as soon as you two are done gluing the papers on."

"I am done," Sara said, standing up and stretching.

Greg glued the last piece of paper on and also stood up and stretched. "I'm done too."

"How do we get to the boat?" Sara asked.

"Simple," Jim said. He pointed at his window. "We can climb out there and down the ladder."

"There's a ladder right outside there?" Greg asked. "Doesn't that look a bit suspicious?"

"It might," Jim said, "if my dad weren't redoing the roof above my room."

"Ah, smart idea," Sara said, and started to climb out the window. She did not have her feet on the ladder yet when there was a knock on Jim's door.

"Jim, can I come in?" his mother asked.

There was not enough time to pull Sara back in to his room. Jim pushed Greg down on the floor and flung himself on to his bed right as his mother opened his door.

Chapter 5

"Here you go," Jim's mother said, putting a plate of warm chocolate chip cookies on his bedside table. "Where's Sara?"

"In the bathroom," Greg said, pretending to glue a piece of paper on to the science project.

"Nice project, but aren't you chilly?" she asked, and then saw the open window. On the very edge, Sara's fingers clung on. Jim could see that from his perspective, but his mother could not.

She started to step forward. "I'll close that for you."

"That's okay mom," Jim said, jumping up, and walking as fast as he could with out causing suspicion over to the window, "I've got it."

"Thanks, Jim," his mother said. "Keep working on your project, it looks great!"

"Thanks, mom," Jim said as the door swung closed. Jim went quickly over to the window and opened it. He grabbed Sara's arm, and helped her over toward the ladder.

"That was close," Jim said. He helped Greg climb out, and then climbed out himself. He closed the window as far as he could without entirely closing it, and climbed down the ladder.

"You got the keys?" Greg asked.

"Yep, right here," Jim said, twirling them around his finger. "The dock's this way. Keep quiet. My parents might be able to hear us until we are on the lake."

They slowly walked through the reeds, until they got to the dock. Greg and Sara climbed in and hid behind two boxes in the bottom of the boat.

Jim turned the ignition, but the boat did not start. He went through all the steps again, and turned the key. A loud pop echoed through the reeds, and Jim saw his mother look out the living room window.

He ducked as low as he could, and put the boat in idle. For what seemed like eternity, his mother looked out the window. Finally, she turned away, and went back to what she was doing.

Jim moved the throttle forward slightly and the boat eased backward. He turned ninety degrees back ward, then slowly switched the motor to forward.

The motor hummed almost silently as the boat pushed through the reeds. The bow searched for Lake Minnetonka as reeds brushed the hull.

"How much longer?" Sara asked, but was quiet when Jim fervently shook his head. He put the boat in neutral and looked back at the house.

The back door had opened and he saw his mother come out the back door. She was headed for the dock.

"I think she's caught us," Jim said. "What do we do now?"

"She's going to be angry," Greg said, "let's just cruise a bit, then come back when she's calmed down."

Jim watched his mother walk closer and closer toward the dock, knowing at any moment she would find the boat missing. Moments before she walked around the bend and saw the boat, she turned and walked in to the shed.

She was in the shed for only a few seconds and came out with a large foldable table. She shut the door to the shed and walked back to the house.

Jim let out a sigh of relief once the back door was closed, and started the boat back in to a slow cruise.

"Are we safe?" Sara asked.

The boat rounded the last of the reeds, and Jim saw the empty lake illuminated by the crescent moon.

"For now," he said, and moved the throttle forward. The boat jumped, and the motor hummed louder. The boat sped off across Lake Minnetonka, jumping in the small waves.

Chapter 6

"I'm going to be seasick if we don't get there soon," Sara said. The boat was jumping higher and higher as the winds had picked up since they had left Jim's house.

All three were huddled down as far as they could get. The wind whipped anything above the level of the windshield around.

Jim was peering over the edge of the dashboard, looking out the windshield as best as he could. He pulled the throttle back as he saw a dock come in to view.

On the end of the dock that stuck out in to the lake a small building was perched. Where the dock met the shore there was a tall gate.

In cursive letters across the top, Jim could read *Bernel's School*. He slowed the boat to a crawl and bent back down. The wind was not nearly as bad now that the boat was stopped and they were all able to look up.

"This is the right place then?" Greg asked, pointing to the gate.

"Yeah," Jim said, pulling the boat alongside the dock. He jumped off and quickly tied the front and back ropes to the dock. He then reached on to the dashboard and grabbed the keys.

He helped Greg and Sara off the boat, and then grabbed the two backpacks from the back. The wind picked up again, and Jim gestured toward the woods.

They ran toward the gate. Jim feared it would be locked, but when he touched the gate, it swung open with ease. They ran in to the woods, and Jim stopped by a tall pine.

"The school can't be far away," he said, looking toward the tall chimney he could see over the trees. "We have to be careful of the guards. The school might have some posted to keep burglars out."

They slowly made their way through the woods, keeping as quiet as they could. Ahead, Jim could here the woodshop machine going.

They finally made it to the edge of the woods and ahead was a large clearing with a gravel parking lot. A lone van sat in the lot, next to the wide open double doors to the wood shop.

Inside, large metal tubes snaked around machines. The machines were a jumble of dull metal, bright red tape and fluorescent yellow paint. With all the lights on, Jim had to squint to see in.

The left side was open and Jim could see Mr. Stevens sanding down a carving of a loon.

Above the woodshop was a balcony. Three sets of double glass doors led out on to the balcony from the art room. Jim pointed up at the balcony.

"Up there?" Sara mouthed, also pointing.

Jim shook his head, and took out a long rope. On one end there was a grapple attached. Jim leaned back, and flung the grapple in the air as soon as Mr. Stevens started the sander.

It clattered on the deck, but slid off with out catching. Greg cast a look of fear at Jim as he prepared to throw it again. Jim let the grapple fly, and it swung nicely over the edge of the balcony.

He tugged on the rope, but it remained taught. Jim started to climb first, using pulleys with flat areas on which to stand. Once he got to the balcony, he climbed over and started to help Sara up.

After Sara was on the balcony, they both coached Greg in to climbing the rope, and helped him get over the edge. The whining of the sander still echoed in the night.

Greg shivered as he said, "I hate heights."

"Let's go," Jim said, waving his arm and walking over to the balcony door. He pulled hard, but the door remained locked shut.

Jim kneeled down and slowly slid a small card along the edge of the door. The lock popped and Jim opened the door. He gestured and let Greg and Sara go in first.

Jim closed the door quietly behind him and made sure to lock it. He was glad to find the door to the art room locked from the outside, but not the inside.

He stuck his head in to the hallway, and thought it was clear. Right before he walked in to the hall a guard came around the corner.

Jim quickly shut the door to the art room, and pushed himself up against a wall. For what seemed like an eternity, the guard's steps echoed down the hall toward them.

Finally, he walked past the door and Jim was able slowly open the door to look at him. He was short, but he looked strong and he had a gun.

Jim silently shut the door as the guard turned around and headed back the way he came. He walked past the door again and it was a short while until Jim said something.

"You guys, I think we'll have to use the air ducts."

"Oh, no," Greg said as he began to breathe faster. "We are going to have to climb back down the balcony."

Chapter 7

Jim unlocked the balcony door, and slowly opened it. The whine of the sander still echoed in the woods. He went over to the edge of the balcony and saw Mr. Steven's blue van below.

"Hurry, before he finishes," Jim said, waving to his friends. "It's already nine-fifteen, and he will probably be leaving soon."

"What are we going to do?" Greg asked.

"Jump," said Sara. She climbed on to the railing, and swung her feet on the outside of the balcony. There was a small lip and Sara put her feet on it.

Mr. Steven's van sat a few feet below her. She let go and fell on to the roof. She then slid off the side and called quietly up at them.

"Hurry, he's starting to shut the equipment off."

"Greg, come on, let's go," Jim said, pulling Greg toward the edge.

"Are you sure it is safe?" Greg asked, his voice quivering slightly.

"Yeah, Sara made it," Jim said, convincing Greg to go over the edge and hang over the van.

The lights in the wood shop were all going off, and Jim could here the vents slowing to a stop.

"Hurry, on the count of three," Jim said.

"Okay," Greg said, preparing himself for the drop.

"One, two, three."

Jim and Greg fell and landed on the roof. There was a heavy thud when they did, but luckily, Mr. Stevens slammed the door to the shop shut at the same time.

Greg was able to slip off the passenger side and in to the woods, but when Jim started to move, Mr. Stevens got in to the van.

Jim knew if he made any quick movement, Mr. Steven would be able to hear him. The van started up and drove under the balcony.

It turned left and started to head up the hill along side the school. Jim was slowly sliding himself backward. He was able to drop his feet over the edge, and finally drop entirely on to the rear bumper.

He saw the corner of the school approaching and knew it would be the only safe place to jump. He saw a flagpole with the school's flag on it hanging on the corner.

He jumped and grabbed on to the flagpole. He watched Mr. Steven drive away, not noticing him. He sighed and dropped from the pole.

"Jim, are you okay?" Sara asked, running out of the woods. Greg followed her closely.

"Yeah, I'm fine. Let's find that vent opening," Jim said, straightening his hat.

"It is right over there," Greg said, pointing past Jim. "Unfortunately, it's right past the main entrance."

"We could walk around," Sara suggested.

"We could," Jim said, "but that would take too long. Let's risk it."

They silently crept past the dark windows, gazing in occasionally. Right past the main entrance was the office area. The main office area was open, and had large plate-glass windows looking out in to the garden area.

Jim kept low, but luckily, they did not see any guards in the main entrance.

"Watch out, though," Jim said. "Remember, they have security cameras. Do not let the cameras see you either."

They went around the corner of the school and finally came to the grate. Greg quickly took a tool case out of his backpack and unscrewed the grate.

He lowered it as quietly as he could. Jim had just crawled inside when a security guard walked around the edge of the building.

Less than twenty feet from Greg and Sara, Jim was sure he could hear their breathing. Jim held his breath and motioned for Greg and Sara to hold their breath also.

The beam from the flashlight hit the bush and kept on moving, making a wide sweep of the area. Jim could not see the guard but was sure the guard would see Greg and Sara.

"I see you," the guard said.

Jim panicked. He did not know what to do. Perhaps he could reason with the guard. If the guard caught all three of them, though, they would not solve the mystery.

Jim decided he could not just save himself and let Greg and Sara deal with the guard. He had to do something. He could not think of something and stayed frozen in the vent.

Jim heard the guard yell, "Come out with your hands in the air or else."

Chapter 8

"I am warning you," the guard shouted. Jim could not move yet, not knowing what he could do, but knowing he had to do something.

"Bring it on, Montebello!" the guard shouted. "Hay, hum, hyah!"

Jim stuck his head out the grate and saw the guard fighting. He was fighting no one, and was doing slow karate moves, like in the movies.

"Hwee, haa, bang! Take that you blubbering mobster," the guard said as he pretended to throw someone in to a dumpster.

Sara was trying as hard as she could not to laugh aloud, while Greg was gesturing frantically at her to be quiet. After some time the guard stopped and continued down the side of the school. Occasionally he would kick out at an invisible mobster.

"Let's go," Greg said, pushing Sara in to the air duct.

Jim ducked his head and crawled a short ways. He took a map out of his back pocket and looked at it carefully.

"This way," he said taking the right vent. A few feet beyond was a large grate like the one outside. As Jim crawled up next to it, he could hear electronic equipment humming.

"This is the right place?" Sara asked, listening. "It seems a little quiet.

"You'd be surprised how quiet computers are nowadays," Greg said. "Even huge ones probably are not as loud as that."

"So, how many do you think there are?" Sara asked as Jim began to unscrew the grate.

"I do not know, nor can I guess how many -," Greg said.

"Oh come on," Sara said.

"- But, I do know it will not be what you expect."

"Well, then I expect it to be six computers," Sara said.

"Really?" Greg said, giving her an odd look. "Five bucks says there is only four."

"You're on!" Sara said, pulling out a small notebook. "Five on number of computers."

She scribbled a note in the notebook, and put it back in her pocket.

Jim was working on the last screw. "This does not want to come out," Jim said, trying to pry it out with a hammer.

"Let me see," Greg said, coming over and pulling on the hammer.

Sara started to lie back in the vent when she slipped a little on the smooth metal. "Wait!"

"What?" Jim and Greg asked together.

Move back here, Sara said, and they all moved back to the vent they had come from. Sara lay on her back and pushed away from the wall with her arms.

She flew down the vent like a bobsledder, Jim and Greg quickly following. She smashed her foot in to the vent, and it cracked, spilling her on to the floor.

Greg looked out the vent first and gazed around. "We're in deep trouble."

Chapter 9

Sara opened her eyes and looked around at the room. Then she began to laugh. She rolled around the floor as Jim gazed disbelieving at the surroundings.

The floor was metal, like in warehouses. The walls were whitewashed concrete. The room was empty, save for one corner.

Two small cubicles were in it. Each had an old Mac running a security program. Each cubicle had the guards' nicknames posted by the entrance, *Mac* and *Johnny*.

Next to the Macs were small monitors, divided in to quarters, which changed every three seconds to show new views of the school.

Sara was finally able to stop laughing and sit up. She gazed around the room and took in what little there was.

"Nice job, Jim," she said, walking over to one of the cubicles. "You brought us here for nothing."

"Maybe, but we would not have known it was nothing if we had not come here," Jim said defensively.

"Really?" Greg asked, walking over to Jim. "I distinctly remember telling you two not to do this. I said there was nothing to find."

"Us two?" Jim asked, going over toward Greg. "I thought it was just Sara's harebrained idea to come here."

"You couldn't just left well enough alone, could you?" Greg said, pushing Jim. "You had to go and waste more of our time. Now, my dad will probably be mad at me. This is just like when you thought Ms. Harcourt was a vampire-"

"Wait, I never said that-"

"We have probably wasted an entire evening, we might get in deep trouble, and it was your idiotic idea,"

"Idiotic?" shouted Jim. "I will show you idiotic."

Jim jumped on Greg and pushed him to the floor. Jim jumped up quickly as Sara leaned back on the desk to watch Jim and Greg go at it. She had never seen Greg so angry.

Sara slipped on a piece of paper and hit a pile of papers hard with her elbow. As she cried out in pain, then floor fell out from below Jim.

Chapter 10

Jim stuck his foot out as it hit a rung. He also grabbed a rung with his right hand. He jerked his arm, but did not fall any further.

Below him, the hole stretched infinitely in to darkness. Sara and Greg leaned over the edge.

"Jim, are you okay?" Sara asked, reaching down to grab his hand.

"Yeah, but that was scary," Jim said, climbing up the ladder and back on to the solid floor of the security room.

"I wonder what a tunnel like that is doing in the floor of the security room," Greg said, leaning over to inspect it. He took out a flashlight and shined it down the hole. "It looks to be about twenty feet deep."

Inherent Legacy

"Wonder what's hidden twenty-feet under the school," Sara said, also leaning over the edge.

"Well," Jim said, grabbing his backpack, "as you two well know, I am not one to let a mystery go unsolved."

"Jim, I would not do that if I were you," Greg said.

Jim stopped climbing down. "You are right, I should probably – No. I feel I have to go on."

Jim again began to climb down the hole.

"He's a lunatic, right?" Greg said, turning to look at Sara. She was gone, already following Jim down the hole. "Wait you guys."

At the bottom of the pit was a small room with concrete walls. They were alike, and the only thing in the room was a small lamp on a small foldable table.

Their footsteps made hollow echoes, along with drips of water coming from pipes above. The darkness surrounded them, and they could barely see the damp walls.

"Well," Sara said, "it leads nowhere. I guess Greg was right, let's head back."

"No, wait," Jim said. "The pipes must lead somewhere. If only we could see better."

He flipped the lamp switch on, but no light came one. Instead, the concrete wall in front of him sunk back and slid to the right.

Ahead of them, the room they were really looking for appeared, and all three gasped.

Chapter 11

Several black towers hummed with electronic processors, and the air smelled of warm metal. In two corners, long L-shaped desks sat with several computers on them.

"This can not all be the school's, can it?" Greg asked.

Jim walked over to one of the computers and read a small help box that popped up. "No, it belongs to a Mr. Vaughn."

"I thought you did not know anything about computers," Sara said.

"I only know one thing, how to bring up the help box," Jim said, laughing.

"I am going to look around," said Greg.

"Okay," said Sara. "Jim, can you open that program and see what it is?"

"Sure, just a second. There you go."

"What is it?" Sara asked.

"It is a program that has been specially designed to track ships on the ocean," Jim said, clicking on a button.

"What is that?" Sara asked a red blip popped up on screen.

"It looks like it is tracking a ship."

"Where?" Sara said impatiently.

"It look's like – well, that is funny," Jim said, clicking several pop-up boxes.

"What is it?" Sara asked.

"The boat is on Lake Minnetonka, and it is a small boat."

"Where's it going?" Sara asked, leaning over Jim's shoulder.

"Excuse me," Jim said, pushing her back. "It is on a route saved as dmpradmat.pfrt. Let me see if I can find any more info."

While Jim was clicking through the information boxes, Sara wrote down the route name.

Inherent Legacy

"Sorry, I cannot find any more information," Jim said, leaning back.

"That is okay," Sara said, "I love a good word riddle."

She leaned over her notebook and quickly tried to separate the name in to two words.

"This one sure is tough," she said, biting the end of her pencil. "Do you know where the boat is now?" Sara asked.

"Yeah, the eastern side of the lake, not far from here," Jim said. He looked at the screen and quickly began to click through different boxes. "I wonder what else is near there."

Sara was busy writing away as Greg worked in the corner. He took a box out of his backpack. It was about the size of a book, and had a microphone-like device attached to it by a cord.

The inside of his backpack was cluttered with tools he had found at pawn shops and garage sales. Most of it was equipment that most people would never think of using.

Greg held up the microphone to a pile of barrels in front of him. The device he was holding issued soft clicks in rapid succession.

"You guys!" Greg called, his voice quivering a bit. "You will never guess what they have hidden back here."

"Not right now," Sara said, and went back to her puzzle.

"I think you should come and see this," Greg insisted.

"What is it?" Jim said, reluctantly standing up from the computer. Sara also reluctantly got up and followed him.

They walked over to stand next to Greg. He was silently staring up at the pile of barrels.

"What is it?" Jim asked impatiently.

Greg continued to stare at the pile as he replied.

"It is three tons of radioactive waste."

Chapter 12

"Radioactive waste?" Jim asked. "Are you sure you did not make a mistake somewhere?"

"Yes, I checked it very carefully, and I am ninety-nine percent sure it's radioactive waste," Greg said. He set his backpack on the concrete floor and put his Geiger counter away. He zipped up, and then shouldered his backpack.

"Do you realize what this means?" Sara asked.

"Yeah," Jim said, "it means –"

At the other end of the room, the door buzzed and slid open. A short, balding man was hobbling on a cane. Next to him walked a younger, much taller man.

"Mr. Vaughn, sir," the taller man said.

"Yes, Matthew?" Mr. Vaughn said, sitting down at a computer at the other end of the room.

"The boat has arrived and will return shortly," Matthew said. He sat down behind Mr. Vaughn and sat quietly while Mr. Vaughn worked.

"Move," Jim whispered quietly to Sara and Greg, pushing them behind the barrels. Mr. Vaughn unexpectedly stood up and walked over toward the barrels.

"Do not breathe," Jim said, as all three lay on the ground.

"You know Matthew, I have been dreaming of this for a long time," Mr. Vaughn said, staring at the pile of barrels much as Greg had.

"Sir, do not forget what you said about being the stereotypical villain."

"I am not a villain, I realized," Mr. Vaughn said. "Like in the books, I am like the unexpected hero who takes on an evil country."

"Yes, sir," Matthew said.

"Revenge, Matthew, must be swift, powerful, and just," Mr. Vaughn said, and then walked back to the computer. "How are the preparations going?"

"The goose is almost caught," Matthew said, heading back after Mr. Vaughn.

"Good, I cannot wait for the prelude."

Jim got on to his hands and knees and crawled over to peer over the barrel. The barrels were damp, and green fuzz covered the edge of one.

"Quick," Jim said, pointing to a grate nearby, "Greg, get working on it.

Greg and Sara shuffled over to the grate and Greg quickly and silently removed it. Jim watched Mr. Vaughn carefully, seeing if he could decipher what he and Matthew were talking about.

"Jim, come on," Greg whispered.

Jim gazed back one more time, longing to know what they were talking about. Then he reluctantly crawled over to the grate, and began to climb up the vertical tube.

Chapter 13

Jim reached up and grabbed Greg's hand as Greg helped pull him over the lip of the duct. Stretched out below him was the twenty-foot chasm they had just climbed up.

The slick metal had made it hard, but they had made it up eventually. Below they could still hear the quiet conversation between Matthew and Mr. Vaughn.

"Mr. Vaughn, we have intruders!" echoed up the vent suddenly, and they heard a siren blaring in the concealed room below them.

"We're in trouble now," Jim said. "Hurry, let's get out of here before they find us."

"Good idea," Greg said. "I think the exit is this way."

They crawled quickly until they finally made it back to where they had started. Again, they saw the guard walk past, but he did not seem to be part of Mr. Vaughn's gang.

"Okay," Greg said, "the coast looks clear, let's go."

They all ran close to the ground along the side of the building and in to the woods. They slowed to a walk, and were relieved when the dock was finally in sight.

Several gunshots echoed through the night, and a large limb landed near them. Jim, looking back and panicking, saw the light from the guards' flashlights coming down the hill.

"Run to the boat!" Jim yelled, and all three ran as fast as they could to the boat. Greg ripped the ropes off their holds, and Jim dove in to the boat and started it.

The engine whirred to life, and Jim quickly backed the boat away from the dock. He did a quick three-point turn and slammed the throttle all the way forward.

As the boat jumped away from the dock, the guards ran on to the dock. They looked dumbfounded for a second, and then the leader leaned over and picked something off the ground.

"They cannot get us now," Sara said as she laughed with joy.

Jim suddenly heard a whirring noise, and saw the building at the end of the dock rising up. Below the building, a large black balloon billowed out.

All four guards jumped on it, and it slid off the dock and in to the water. That is when Jim realized that it was not a building. It was a hovercraft.

"Hold on!" Jim yelled, pushing the boat even faster. The hovercraft was catching up, and Jim knew they could not go faster than it could.

Sara and Greg had seen the hovercraft and were looking back at it. Both had wide eyes, and were too scared to do anything.

After flying around the lake for several minutes, Jim did not know where they were. Suddenly, ahead of him he saw a bridge. On it, he could read *Gray's Bay Causeway*.

Jim glanced back and saw a guard pull something large out of the hovercraft. Turning the wheel hard, a large rocket barely missed them and exploded on the bridge.

Chunks of the side of the bridge fell in to the lake. Jim noticed that when the hovercraft tried to turn, it slid and slowed dramatically.

He turned sharply again and sped away from the bridge, heading back the way they had come. He was looking for one of the docks near the school. He knew several of the school's neighbors.

If he could find one, he might be able to find some help. Next to the boat, there was another explosion and water swamped the boat.

Jim panicked and fell to the left. He hit the wheel, and the boat went in to a long, wide curve. Standing back up quickly, he regained control.

However, it was too late. Just thirty feet ahead was a dock. Jim tried to turn right. The boat did not make it. The left side of the boat hit the dock.

It spun sideways in the air, flying over the dock. Jim, Greg and Sara fell out and splashed in to the lake next to the dock. Jim surfaced in time to see the boat hit a barrel of gasoline at the end of the dock.

Ducking back under water, a huge explosion burned the dock, and mangled the boat. The hovercraft hit the burned dock and spun head over heels.

It got thirty feet high and over the wreckage of Jim's boat. It crashed in to the low branches of a pine. Jim pulled himself on to what remained of the dock, and ran to the boat.

He grabbed all of the supplies he could find. By the time he did, Sara and Greg had pulled themselves on to shore. Jim ran over, and handed Greg his backpack.

"My dad's not going to be happy," Jim said, looking at the boat. "Come on; let's go back to the school before they can send more guards to get us."

They ran off in to the woods, back toward the school. Matthew crawled out of the wreckage and picked up his radio.

"Da... Mr. Vaughn. They are headed back to the school."

Chapter 14

"I cannot believe it," Greg said, shaking a small black box. "Ruined. It says here this is supposed to be waterproof too."

"Yeah, but bomb proof?" Sara asked, giving a slight chuckle.

Their voices echoed slightly in the vents, and they were trying to stay as quiet as possible. They had already heard several guards searching for them. However, no one even seemed to think about looking in the vents.

"Mr. Vaughn said to look very carefully, they took something important," a guard said. His voice echoed down the vent. Again, they sat as quiet as they could until the voices had faded away.

"What do we do now?" Sara said, wringing out her shirt.

"Well, I think we might be able to squeeze through the gaps in the gate. Then we could, um," Jim stalled, thinking hard.

"Do what?" Greg asked. "Do you honestly believe someone will listen to you if you run in to a police screaming, 'There is a secret base under my school'?"

"Well, it might work," Sara said, defending Jim.

"Yeah, but more likely then not you would be thrown in to the nut house."

Again, they heard voices approaching and quieted down.

"You idiot! You are supposed to guard the perimeter!" one guard yelled at the other. "How could you let three teenagers slip past you?"

"I do not know, I was watching carefully," the other guard said as they walked away.

"Yeah, for the mobster guy," Sara said rolling her eyes.

"Come on," Greg said, getting on his hands and knees. "The gate idea is the best one we have right now. We might as well try it."

Greg and Sara set off down the vent as Jim threw the map he had been drying out in to the back pocket. He zipped it off and crawled after Greg and Sara.

As they rounded a corner, Sara's shoelace was hooked on a small piece of metal that was sticking out. She stopped and tried to pull it loose.

"Let me help you," Jim said, crawling toward her.

A bright light shined in his face as Sara's flashlight went up. Sara fell backwards in to a downward sloping vent. She screamed and Jim dove for her foot.

He missed her foot and slid down the vent right after her.

"Wait for me!" Greg shouted, jumping after them.

For what seemed like eternity, they slid down the vent. Then suddenly Jim saw Sara hit something in front of her. Unable to stop, Jim and Greg right behind him hit Sara and they all tumbled out of the vent and in to thin air.

Jim felt himself falling in to a vast dark cavern and knew that when he hit, he would be lucky if he did not break all his bones. He heard Sara hit the ground below him. He braced for the landing.

Chapter 15

With a light poof, Jim landed on a large, soft mound. His flashlight hit next to him and he grabbed for it. Switching it on, he gazed around.

"Greg! Sara! Are you guys alright?"

"Yeah, we are fine," Sara said from behind him. "Well mostly."

Jim turned around and saw Sara on a mound of gymnastics mats. Greg was holding his ankle tightly.

"Greg, are you okay?" Jim asked.

"Yeah, but I would be better if Sara had not landed on me," Greg said.

"I already said I was sorry, jeez," Sara said, crossing her arms. Then she leaned over and helped him stand up.

Putting his arm around both their shoulders, they were able to climb down off the mats and in to a corner. After they set Greg down, Jim looked at the open vent in the ceiling.

"Well, we cannot go back that way," he said. He took out the map that Greg had given him. The ink was running together and Jim could hardly read it.

"Sara, where's your map?" Jim asked.

"Here," Sara said, handing him her map. It was also smudged, but at least somewhat readable.

A large pounding echoed through the gym.

"We know you are in there," a guard called out from beyond the door. "We are coming in."

Jim heard the guard running at the door and hit it hard with his shoulder.

"Oww! That hurt," the guard yelled.

"Maybe it is locked," his partner said.

"No, really?" the other guard said, standing up. "You kids have to the count of ten to come out."

"What should we do?" asked Sara, panicking slightly.

"One! Two! Three!" the guard shouted from the hallway.

"Come on," Jim said, climbing up the volleyball net pole. "We can get through the balcony door."

"What about Greg?" Sara asked.

Jim looked at Greg and saw that he was looking healthy enough.

"Bring him over. I will climb up the pole, and then you help him up to me," Jim said. He quickly scaled the pole by using the hooks as steps. He reached down with one hand while holding on to the railing with the other.

"Six! Seven!" the guard continued to yell.

"Come on, help him up," Jim said, hurrying Sara so they could escape. Greg put his good foot on the right hand hook and began to pull himself up with Jim's help.

"Eight! Ten!" the guard yelled. A huge explosion rocked the gym and the door flew halfway across it. The guard ran in to the dark cavern and shot randomly around.

Greg screamed as a bullet hit him and he fell on to Sara. The guard saw a flicker of Jim's flashlight and started heading towards them.

"Sara, come on," Jim called. "You have to forget about Greg for now. Come on!"

"I can't, Jim, he's..."

"Sara, just save yourself."

"I can't just leave him."

More gunshots rang out in the dark gym.

"Sara, please. You can't save him if your dead. We can rescue him, I promise."

Reluctantly, Sara turned away from Greg and ran up the pole. Slipping as quietly as they could through the foldable chairs, they got to the balcony door.

Jim slowly opened it and they snuck out in to the hall. It was empty. Jim beckoned to Sara and they both quietly went to the far end of the hall.

"See that door?" Jim asked. "It leads outside, and it will only be a few more minutes until we can get help, okay?"

Sara just shook her head as the rest of her body was shaking. Jim also nodded silently and looked back at the door.

"Hopefully, we will be able to save Greg. Come on, the coast is clear."

They both snuck over to the door and silently opened it. Jim looked out. A slight breeze was coming from the north and Jim shivered instinctively.

He waved to Sara and they both walked crouched to the ground over in to the garden. The plants were high enough to protect them from the sight of the guards and Jim quickly made his way through the garden.

He stopped at the edge of the garden. About one hundred yards away was the gate to freedom. Jim turned back to look at Sara.

"Ready? We will run on the count of three," he said, but Sara was not listening. She was not looking at him. She was not behind him. He was all alone.

"Sara?" He called in to the garden.

A hand covered his face with a handkerchief and Jim felt the world around him fade to black.

Chapter 16

"Are you okay?" a voice said out of the mist.

A blurry world came almost back into focus around Jim. He was in a small closet. In front of him, a short man sat on a foldable chair, typing on a laptop. He had dark black hair, and was wearing a polo shirt and khakis.

The man finished typing something and turned to Jim. He looked young, almost as if he had just graduated from college. He was neat looking and Jim thought he had seen him before.

"Are you okay?" he asked again. "I am sorry about that."

"About what?" Jim asked, looking around. Sara lay on a cot near his. "Who are you, what did you do?"

"Again, I am sorry," the young man said. "It is the only way I could have stopped you from being caught."

Suddenly it hit Jim where he had seen the young man before. "You are the janitor."

"Well, that is my disguise," the man said. "My name is Mr. Thompson, and I am a C.I.A. agent. I have been investigating these people for almost a year."

Thompson went back to the computer and typed a few more sentences. Jim leaned forward enough to see he was typing a document in a text editor.

Thompson typed the last sentence, saved the document, and shut off the laptop. Picking up a tool belt, he snapped it on and grabbed a set of keys off the table.

"What do you know about them dumping the radioactive waste?" Jim asked, climbing off his cot.

"Well, I cannot tell you much," Thompson said. "You can only know that they are not actually dumping toxic waste. "

"They are not?" Jim asked. "What are they doing?"

"I will tell you after I have dealt with them. Right now they are starting the transport, and I must get going," Thompson said. He walked out the door and closed it behind him.

Jim ran after him, but he was not able to open the door before Thompson locked it with a click. Jim backed up and sat on the edge of the cot.

"Jim, Jim?" Sara asked, rubbing her eyes and sitting up. "Whoa, I do not feel good. "Did the bad guys catch us?"

"No," Jim said, "but they should have. The guy who locked us in here is a U.S. spy and he is trying to catch them."

"We are in good hands then?" Sara asked, standing up and stretching.

"Not exactly. I do not think he is very good," Jim said, walking over to the chair and sitting down.

"Why not?" Sara asked, sitting on the cot opposite.

"Well, for one thing, he left his gun right here next to the laptop," Jim said.

"Don't touch it!" Sara blurted out.

"I was not going to," Jim said, looking at her funny.

"I'm sorry," Sara said.

"Why?" Jim asked

"My mother, Sandra, she was shot by a gun. No one knows whom; it was during a bank robbery. There was a good security photo of the man, but no one identified him."

"I am the one who should be sorry," said Jim.

"No, he should," Sara said, pointing to a picture on the wall. A collage of eight men was on the wall. She was pointing to a man in the center.

"Hunter Fields," Jim read off the collage. "Why?"

"He is the guy in the security photo, I know," Sara said. "Come on, let's get out of here, and get him. This is personal now."

She picked up one of the cots and ran the length of the room in to the door. One of the hinges popped off and Jim watched as she did it again.

The third time the door fell down hard on the marble floor and Jim worried that the guards might hear them. Sara did not even seem to notice, though.

"Come on," Sara said, climbing over the wreckage and out in to the hall. Jim grabbed the gun and threw it in a toolbox. Then he threw the toolbox in the backpack.

"I am glad to leave there," Jim said. "I was starting to feel claustrophobic."

"Come on," Sara said, turning to the left and walking past the main entrance. "The office is right over here."

"Sara, wait," Jim said. "What if they are expecting you to come through the office after Thompson?"

"Oh, they aren't," Sara said, hurrying ahead. She peeked through the glass on the side of the door to the office. "See, it is all clear."

She swung open the door and walked in. A large man came up behind her and pushed a bag over her head. He wrapped it around her and picked her up.

"Let me out! Help!" Sara cried from the bag. Jim desperately fought the urge to go rescue her, because if he did, they would catch him also.

Carrying her with him, the large guard descended down the ladder as Jim ran out the front door and around to the vent.

Chapter 17

Jim coughed quietly as he slowly descended the vertical vent he had climbed up several hours ago. It seemed like several days to him.

"Well, is that all?" Mr. Vaughn's voice echoed up the vent.

"Yes, sir," Jim heard a guard say. "We have caught all three of them."

"Well, Mr. Thompson," Mr. Vaughn said, "I see we are having some trouble keeping secretive. Ha ha ha!"

Jim lowered the grate to the floor and crawled out on to the concrete. He heard Mr. Vaughn still talking to Thompson. He took out the gun, and then stopped.

He looked the gun over, thinking of why it was made. He did not want to be a murderer and join the ranks of his enemies. He did not want to kill anyone.

He picked up the gun. He raised it high in the air. Then he threw it as far as he could across the room. It clattered and banged in to computers and other stuff.

Jim looked over the barrel, preparing to surrender when he saw the rest of the room. It was empty. Mr. Vaughn and his guards had taken his friends through the door at the end.

Jim ran over to the door, but it was made of smooth concrete. He could not get a good grip on it. Next to the door was a security code pad, but Jim did not know any.

He fell backward against the wall in to a sitting position. He could not think of how to save Sara, Greg, and Thompson now. He was locked on the room with no escape.

"Sara would probably want to look for a rocket launcher and blow the door down," Jim said, laughing a little. "Greg would probably know the codes. He can learn anything by just looking it up on his-"

Jim stopped as the realization hit him. He could look up the codes on the computers. There were several in the room with him.

He ran over to one and furiously began to scroll through the help programs. He finally found the one he was looking for, one called List Code.

It asked for Jim's user name and password.

"Well, Mr. Vaughn cannot be that different from everyone else," Jim reasoned. He typed in Vaughn for the user name and vaughn1 for the password.

"Would you like to print a reference copy of this chart?" a pop-up box asked Jim. He clicked 'Yes' and the printer next to the computer hummed and printed a copy of what was on the screen.

Jim went over to the door and punched in the code. He stood around the edge of the door in case Mr. Vaughn and his men were just around the corner.

He glanced for a second around the corner, but everything was clear. The next room looked like an underground parking garage with parking spaces for five small golf carts.

Three were gone, but two remained parked in their spaces. Six tunnels branched off from the garage, but only one had on the fluorescent lights that lit it.

He looked in the cart and saw a set of keys dangling in the ignition. Jim threw his backpack in the back seat, jumped in the driver's seat, and sped off down the tunnel after his friends.

Chapter 18

The fluorescent lights flickered past overhead as Jim drove down the tunnel. It curved and wound, forcing Jim to pay attention.

Jim had a hard time paying attention, though, because he had not had any sleep the whole night long. His watch read 4:32 AM, and he desperately wanted to sleep.

Thinking of his friends and Mr. Thompson, though, always made him straighten up and keep on driving. No matter how blurred the lights became, Jim always tried to pay close attention

He was paying close enough attention to notice the tunnel starting to slope upward he slowed his cart down even more and rolled in to the end garage.

He saw the three other carts parked next to each other and saw a concrete door off to the right. Parking his cart next to the others, he grabbed his backpack and jumped out.

He ran over to the door and pulled out his code sheet. Quickly punching in the code, he made a mistake and the door only beeped back at him.

He tried again, this time forcing himself to slow down. The door beeped again, but this time the door slid open. A vertical shaft led up toward a hatch about thirty feet above him.

Jim slung his backpack over his shoulder, grabbed a rung, and began to climb. When he got to the hatch, he slowly lifted it up slightly until he could see out.

He was in a small, dark room with a light source behind him. He decided to risk it and climb out of the hole. He looked around after he got out and saw he was in a ticket booth of some kind.

He looked out the open window and saw a large open area with glass walls beyond. A staircase partially obstructed his view, but he could tell where he was just the same.

He was in the Hopkins Center for the Arts. Across the street to the right, the bright lights of the Hopkins theatre shone, even though it was closed.

Jim hopped silently over the counter and stole down the hall to the right. He stopped in front of the locked door to the offices, where the wall started to curve. On the right was whitewashed walls, curving out to the left, then flattening.

On the left were the curved glass windows looking out on to an empty Main Street. In front of the theatre doors, Jim saw Sara, Greg, and Thompson tied to chairs with Mr. Vaughn and three guards standing around them.

"Mr. Vaughn, are you crazy?" Sara shouted, figuring out how to move the gag out of her mouth.

"No, why?" Mr. Vaughn asked, scowling at her.

"Tying people to chairs, how stereotypical," Sara said. "You could not even think of anything smarter."

"Ah, but of course not," Mr. Vaughn said. "I decided to get rid of my stupid prey in a stupid fashion."

"That makes no sense," Sara said. "You are a total luna-"

One of the guards put Sara's gag back in and tightened it.

Mr. Vaughn leaned over her and said, "Too bad, I guess you are just a sore loser."

Sara rocked her chair back and forth, trying to hit him, but could not. The guards just laughed at her, and the tallest one leaned over.

He took a large briefcase out of a larger bag and set it in front of Thompson. He flicked a small switch, and stepped back.

"So, Mr. Thompson, I will now leave you. You only have about ten minutes to sunrise, so do not worry," Mr. Vaughn said. "Oh, wait! How could I forget to introduce you to my friend?"

He leaned over the briefcase and stroked it as if it was a cat.

"This is a dirty bomb," Mr. Vaughn. "Keep it out of the sunlight, or else it can get very *explosive*. Ha ha! Bye, bye now."

Mr. Vaughn turned and walked toward Jim. Not knowing what to do, Jim ran backward as fast as he could. He quickly and quietly opened a large door and slipped in to the room.

He was surrounded by paintings. It was a special gallery of students' artwork from around the city. He heard Mr. Vaughn and his guards go out the front door.

Inherent Legacy

Jim stuck his head out the door and saw them walking slowly down the street. Mr. Vaughn seemed very cheerful by stopping at every store window to look at the merchandise.

Jim slipped out of the room and ran down the hall to Sara, Greg, and Thompson. He quickly cut the ropes with his knife, started to look at the bomb.

"What are you looking for?" Greg asked, leaning over.

"There has got to be some way to deactivate it, right?" Jim asked.

"Just a second, I think I might, be able to deactivate it" Greg said, leaning over the bomb and slowly lifting off a plate.

Sara was helping Thompson get untied from the chair, but he was not doing well. She was trying to pull it off, but he kept getting it tangled.

"I'm so sorry I got caught, I couldn't help it. That man killed Sandra," Thompson said.

"Who?" Jim asked.

"Sandra, she was my partner."

"Hold still," Sara said. She pulled hard on the chair, and the roped ripped off Thompson. She used too much force, though, and the chair flew out of her hands and through the window.

Jim looked up quickly and saw Mr. Vaughn and his guards running back down the street.

"Run!" shouted Jim.

Chapter 19

"Run!" Jim shouted again.

Greg grabbed the bomb and slid it carefully in to his backpack. Sara pulled Thompson after Greg and Jim. They ran down to the end of the curved hallway.

Jim pushed open a set of double doors, and turned to the right quickly. He ran through another set of double doors and took a quick left.

Ahead lay a dead end hallway. As Thompson, Sara, and finally Greg caught up with him, he could hear Mr. Vaughn yelling at his guards.

Jim swung open the second door on his left, noticing it was the green room. Inside, however, there was no green. Several old couches lay around.

On a round table at one end was a basket with a half-empty water bottle in it. Jim ran over and picked up the table with all his strength.

Greg also ran over and began to help Jim lift the table up. Greg's ankle still was swollen, and sore. He groaned as they tilted the table on its side. Jim nodded his head at the window, and Greg nodded back.

They could hear Mr. Vaughn and his men searching back stage for them. Sara and Thompson were ready to jump out the window after them as soon as they broke through.

"Go," Jim said, and he and Greg threw the table through the window. It crashed through the glass, shattering it all over the sidewalk outside.

Jim jumped out of the window and ran to the right down the sidewalk. The rest of them followed him closely. Jim ran like there was no other choice, which there was not.

"Where are you going?" Thompson asked, catching up to Jim.

"Greg's house," Jim said, pointing across the large open park ahead of them. "His house is right over then hill there. The hill is a trail."

The park consisted of a large open-air building in the center with baseball fields on three corners and a football field on the far left one.

"Duck!" Jim shouted, seeing Mr. Vaughn run out of the Hopkins Center for the Arts. He pushed all three of them down the ten-foot embankment.

He pulled Sara up and Greg pulled Thompson up. They ran as fast as they could across the parking lot and down the asphalt path. They were fenced in between the fences of two of the baseball fields.

They ran past the building and ducked behind it. Again, shots rang out, but the building protected them. Ahead was a twenty-foot embankment.

On top of it was a trail. On the other side was Greg's house, and help. Near the edge of the path was a five-foot retaining wall built to stop the path from deteriorating.

Jim ran ahead of the group and leapt over the retaining wall with ease. He slid down to his stomach and turned to help Sara. She was already up though, and running across the path.

"I am going to go get some help," Sara shouted, sliding down the opposite side of the trail.

Jim turned to see Greg running up the hill. Thompson lagged far behind him, wearily trying to get up the hill. Jim reached his hand down and helped Greg make it on to the path.

Behind Thompson, Jim could see Mr. Vaughn and his guards already halfway across the park.

"Come on!" Jim shouted to Thompson. Thompson wearily made it to the wall and Greg and Jim helped him up.

"Let's go," Greg said. "Sara is getting help."

They started to run across the trail. Just before they got to the edge, Jim heard a machine gun cock behind him.

"Down!" Jim shouted, pushing Greg and Thompson down the steep side of the embankment.

Chapter 20

Jim slid down the embankment after Greg and Thompson. Above dirt sprayed up where the bullets had hit the path. It looked like they were going to be safe until Thompson hit the road,

He hit his leg hard and the road, and Jim heard something in his foot crack. Greg heard it too, and they both picked him up and hobbled him over toward Greg's house.

Sara came running out the door. She was crying.

"Jim, Greg, they are gone," she cried.

"Who?" Jim and Greg asked together.

"Your parents," Sara said to Greg. "All of our parents are gone. They are probable looking for us!"

"Well, we can call the police," Jim said.

"They will not get here in time," Greg pointed out as they helped Thompson in to the house.

"I've got it," Jim said, handing Thompson the phone. "Call the police, explain the situation. We will distract them until the police arrive."

"Where are you going?" Thompson asked as Jim ran out the back door.

"We are headed toward Country Village," Jim said. "Greg, Sara, grab your bikes, we are going on a wild goose chase."

Chapter 21

Jim, Sara, and Greg swung left around the corner. Glancing to his right quickly, Jim saw Mr. Vaughn and two of his guards steal and hop on to three bikes.

Jim, Sara, and Greg were all riding the bikes that were stored in Greg's shed.

The third guard was left alone in the alley, while his fellow guards chased after Jim, Greg, and Sara. When Jim got to the first road, he took a right on to the sidewalk.

Greg turned on to the sidewalk also, but Sara was too slow and ended up on the street. Pedaling as fast as they could, Jim saw the path ahead with the park beyond. Right past the path, Jim turned down the steep hill, followed closely by Greg and Sara.

He flew across the grass, bumping up and down, hitting several yellow dandelions in the grass. He held on to his bars tightly, not wanting to fall and be caught.

Mr. Vaughn and the guard next to him were on large red bikes. They belonged to Greg's neighbor, who was a professional bike rider. The second guard, however, was squatting precariously on top of a little boy's blue bike.

Pedaling even faster, Jim flew across the park and up the steep hill at the opposite end. They came up right next to the path, and flew on to it.

Right behind them, Mr. Vaughn, and a guard also flew over the hill and swerved on to the path. The second guard missed the path and flew in the upper branches of a large pine planted below the path in someone's yard.

Jim coasted through several empty intersections, but the next was Hopkins Crossroad. Several large delivery trucks were already driving past, as Hopkins Crossroad is a main road, preparing to deliver the goods for the day.

Jim did not want to leave the path, because then the guards would have the advantage. He kept on pedaling across the large green area before the road.

Around him, the houses got closer and closer, funneling him toward Hopkins Crossroad. He sped up even more as he neared the main artery of Hopkins. Greg and Sara were on either side of him.

Right behind him Mr. Vaughn and a guard raced, trying to catch them. Ahead the traffic was thick, and a delivery truck was parked right in the crosswalk.

Jim just pedaled harder, and at the last second, the truck moved, and the road was open. Jim, Sara, Greg, Mr. Vaughn, and his guard all flew across the road.

Seconds later a semi-truck, horn blaring, flew through the crosswalk. Jim did not notice, however, that the guards continually blocked them in more and more. The path now had a large white fence on the left separating it from the residential area.

On the right was a split rail wooden fence separating it from a car dealership. Ahead, there was a small dip and curve in the path.

Beyond was an old train bridge. Sara pulled ahead of Jim, and Greg pulled even with him.

Just as they jumped off the dip, a small explosion hit the back of Greg's bike, sending him tumbling through the air. Jim flew sideways in to the metal side of the bridge.

Jim stood up immediately as the guard did not turn fast enough and hit the fence on the ends of the bridge. The tree tangled him up, so he could not get down.

Greg landed hard on the edge of the bridge and rolled. Jim ran after him as Mr. Vaughn skidded to a stop. Jim reached and grabbed Greg's hand right before Greg fell off.

Greg fell still, but was able to get better footing on the edge of the bridge.

"Do not look down," Jim said.

"Jim, help!" Sara cried. Jim spun his head around to see Sara and Mr. Vaughn fighting, Sara desperately trying to protect Greg.

Jim turned to ask Greg if he had his footing when he saw an awful problem. The bomb was slipping out of Greg's backpack.

"Greg, the bomb!" Jim shouted.

"No!" Sara yelled. She hit Mr. Vaughn hard in the stomach and ran over to the edge.

"I've got it!" Greg yelled. He let go of Jim's hand and grabbed the bomb. Jim fell backward as Sara jumped over him and grabbed the handle on top of Greg's backpack.

Greg was leaning far over the edge of the bridge, but Jim jumped up and helped Sara pull him back to the edge.

"That was close," Greg said, hugging the bridge for support.

"Hurry," Jim said, "figure out how to disarm the bomb."

"It's easy," Greg said. "I only have to remove the core, but it is dangerous."

Mr. Vaughn stood back up and ran at them.

"Sara, help Greg," Jim said, and ran back at Mr. Vaughn. Jim grabbed Mr. Vaughn's left arm with both of his hands. Jim swiveled to the right.

With Mr. Vaughn's arm over his left shoulder, Jim lifted him up and threw him over his shoulder. Mr. Vaughn landed hard on the gravel path.

As Jim looked up, he yelled loud, "No!"

Sara turned her head to see the same thing that Jim did. The large red sun was rising in the east, silhouetting the Country Village sign.

Chapter 22

Mr. Vaughn lifted his head up and grabbed Jim's leg, pulling it hard. Jim fell backwards on to the path. He heard a large crack in his head as he hit the path.

Colors flashed in front of his eyes and the world seemed to clone it self shortly. Jim snapped back to his senses immediately as he heard Sara yelling.

"Jim, help! He's going to make it explode!"

Jim sat up and ran over to the edge of the bridge. The bright sun behind him was already shining rays of light through the morning fog.

The only area of darkness was behind the bridge. Greg and Mr. Vaughn both had a hold of the bomb. They were fighting over it. Sara was holding her nose, which was bleeding.

Jim leapt over the side of the bridge, and pulled with Greg. Mr. Vaughn lost his footing shortly, and Jim was able to get the bomb away from him.

"I just need one more second," Greg said, leaning over the bomb.

Jim pushed Mr. Vaughn, and one of his feet swung out away from the bridge. Jim almost lost his footing too, but regained his balance.

Mr. Vaughn suddenly leapt on to the two-foot wide side of the bridge and jumped past Jim. He grabbed the bomb from Greg.

Holding the bomb below the edge with one hand, he threw Greg over the edge with the other.

"Now for you," Mr. Vaughn said, scowling at Jim. "The only way for you to go is with me."

He began to lift the bomb up to the light.

"No!" Jim screamed. He grabbed the bomb and pushed it down my doing a handstand. He began to fall sideways on to the bridge.

Jim looked up and hit Mr. Vaughn it the face. Jim fell over the edge of the bridge and back on to the path as Mr. Vaughn fell on to the highway below.

A bright flash of white light lit up the surrounding area more than the sun and a huge explosion rocked Minnetonka and Hopkins.

PART 2

Six weeks later...

Chapter 1

The bus bounced over the cracks in the road, Jim bouncing with it. He had to go to a *public* school for the rest of the year while Thompson investigated at *Bernel's*.

He was angry at that, but was glad to be alive. They had lived because Greg had...

Jim winced, he could not think of Greg. He and Sara had a huge fight the day after the explosion. The next Wednesday, Greg did not come to school.

On Friday, Jim got a letter from Greg saying his family was moving to California. Greg said he would write another letter in a few days.

Now it was five weeks later, and still no letters.

"Can I sit next to you?" a seventh grader asked timidly.

"Fine, what ever," Jim said as the bus sped around the corner and out of the school parking lot.

"I know a magic trick, want to see?" the seventh grader asked, a wide grin splitting across his face.

"No!" Jim yelled, and turned to look out the window. A few seconds later, he glanced briefly back. The seventh grader was hunched over, staring at the ground.

"I'm sorry," Jim said. "My friend did a magic trick to me today, and I got in trouble."

"Don't worry, it's just a short one." The seventh graders smile lit up his face again.

He took out a penny and placed it on his fingertips. He slowly moved his hand around it and snapped his fingers. The penny almost instantly shot up his sleeve.

Jim did a polite clap. "That was very good."

"Thanks, want to see another?"

Jim was getting sad; the kid was shy and liked magic. He was an exact younger duplicate of Greg.

"Why not?" Jim asked, though, cheerfully smiling.

The seventh grader did the same thing, but instead of snapping his fingers this time, he lifted his hand away. Jim just looked at his hand for a moment.

The seventh grader snapped his fingers, and the penny disappeared from his hand. The bus screeched to a halt at the first bus stop. The seventh grader got up and got off the bus as Jim went back to staring out the windows.

When the bus pulled up to his stop, he slowly trodded down the steps and across the road. A black SUV turned the corner behind him and slowed to a stop.

A man jumped out, and ran at Jim.

"Listen kid, all we want is the code!"

Jim looked at the bus, but it had already pulled away.

"Give it to us and we won't hurt you."

Swiveling away from the man, he jumped on to an air conditioning unit, and on to a neighbor's roof.

Running across it, he heard two more men get out of the SUV. He glanced back in time to see them all pull out long swords.

As he was staring at the silver blades glistening in the sun, he tripped on the gutter, and fell off the roof in to the grass. The attackers followed.

Chapter 2

    Jim rolled as he hit the ground, and sprinted down the sloping yard toward the lake. He and Kyle, a kid who lived in the neighborhood, had built a raft that they could reach by stepping on a long trail of small buoys.

    Jim ran across the dock, and jumped off the end. He landed on the first buoy, and kept jumping. He heard his followers stop at the end of the dock.

    None of them was daring enough to follow, or so Jim hoped. Unfortunately, he was wrong. One was either brave enough, or crazy enough, to follow.

Inherent Legacy

When he made it on to Jim's small raft, he swung his blade down and sliced the wood down the middle. Jim moved slowly back and forth to keep his half from tipping.

The guard tried to row his half of the raft toward Jim, but that's when he discovered how the raft stayed in one place. It was anchored on his side to a large anchor Jim had found at that spot a few years ago.

Jim picked up the oar that was on his side and quickly rowed as far from the dock as he could. After almost a minute, his raft bumped in to something behind him.

He fell backwards on to his family's dock. At the end of the dock on the right was the new red speedboat that the government had purchased for them after Mr. Vaughn's guards had destroyed the old one.

Tied up next to it was a pontoon boat the government had also bought them for helping catch Mr. Vaughn. On his left, he saw his white house perched on the hill.

He heard splashing and yelling coming from his friend's dock, so he quickly jumped to his feet and ran over to the glass sliding door. He tugged hard on the handle.

It remained shut. Inside, Jim could see the lock slide was closed. He searched through his backpack, but only found the keys to Sara's house.

Dang!, he thought. He was supposed to go over to Sara's house. He quickly threw the key back in the bag and ran around front. Diving behind the large plants in front of his house, he dug in the ground, searching for something.

Finally, he lifted up the garage door opener. He tugged on it, but it was stuck. His dad had chained it deep in the ground. He accidentally pressed the button and heard the door open.

"What was that?" a guard yelled from down the street.

"It came from over here."

Jim heard them running, and tensed, ready to run.

Finally, he heard the warning beep come from the garage. He was in the bushes in front of the living room. The garage was fifty feet away.

Jim paused for a second.

The door clicked, and it seemed to reverberate to Jim.

It seemed as if the world was in slow motion.

The door was going down.

The guards were running at him.

He ran.

Across the sidewalk, over the hedge. He sprinted around the corner of the house.

He slid under the door. It barely missed smashing him.

A second later, the bullets hit the door.

Jim ran in to the house and in to the basement.

He ran in to the secret bunker.

Three minutes later, the house blew up.

Chapter 3

Sara almost fell off her new bike as she flew around the corner. She was going fast. She had to lean far over to turn around the corner. She was leaning so far over that her pedals scraped against the road.

Ahead she saw a fifty-foot deep crater where Jim's house used to be. In the middle of it, all she saw was a gray block. She heard sirens in the distance, heading toward the house.

Biking over the edge of the crater and down in, she headed for the gray block. On top was a two-foot thick door that swung open slowly. She could see Jim struggling to open it.

"Jim, are you alright?" Sara asked, hopping off her bike.

"Yeah," he said grunting. The door reached ninety degrees and swung down with a humongous crash. "Let's get out of here."

"We need to call Mr. Thompson," Sara said, standing her ground.

Above on the rim of the crater a black van pulled up.

"Already have," Jim said climbing the slope.

The door slid open and a young man in his twenties stepped out. He was wearing a suit with dark glasses and a gun holstered on his side.

"Jim, Sara, get up here, hurry," he called, reaching his hand down to help Jim out.

"What do we do?" Jim asked, ducking his head and climbing in to the van.

"I have to transport you to a holding place for an hour until I can approve a room at the Protection Center."

Mr. Thompson helped Sara in, and then got in himself. The rear portion of the van was open and carpeted, with benches on either side. Jim and Sara sat on one bench and Mr. Thompson sat on the other.

"Where's this Protection Center?" Sara asked as the van jolted to a start.

They were able to see out the dark back windows. The police pulled up to the crater moments before they drove around the corner.

"It's right near my office, so I'd be able to update you on what's happening."

They sat in silence for several minutes until the van suddenly stopped. Mr. Thompson slid open the door and Jim could see the holding place just outside.

It was a normal white and gray building that no one would think to look for them in. Across the top, the stone read *Hopkins Library*.

Chapter 4

Jim sat at the computer at the front of the library, looking out the window every ten seconds. He typed in searches, but kept misspelling words.

Mr. Thompson had been gone almost two hours, and Jim still had not heard word from Sara yet. She had gone to get some clothes from her house almost an hour and a half ago.

He was nervous, but not too nervous to notice when a large man walked in to the library. Jim had seen him just three hours earlier. He was the guard who had chased him at the bus stop.

Jim inconspicuously stood up and walked toward the back of the library. The guard was looking at the faces in the computer cubicles.

The computers were located behind the checkout, which was right in front of the doors.

To the left was the children's and teen's sections, where Jim was. To the back left were the non-fiction books.

"Can I help you?" the librarian asked.

"No, I was just looking for, um, an open computer," the guard lied.

The librarian looked at him oddly, but went back to checking in books.

Jim slid around the edge of the bookshelf and quickly dashed to the back of the library. He peeked through the shelves and saw the guard heading for the children's section.

The entire library was one floor, and in the back, there was a small cubicle like area with a computer, a reading chair, and a window. Outside the window was a small alley.

Jim sat down at the computer, and pretended to be searching for something. Slowly, the guard made his way through each row. He looked between books, as if Jim might be able to hide between them.

Jim noticed that the guard was making continuous progress toward his temporary shelter. He glanced down the center aisle toward the front door. Outside he was able to see the guard's black SUV.

Jim stood up and purposely knocked a book on the ground. Bending over, he grabbed the chair base, instead of the book. He stood quickly up, and threw the chair out the window.

The crash echoed through the small, quiet library. The librarians came running. The guard also came quickly. Jim hopped on to the window edge, and jumped in to the alley.

Running as fast as he could toward the end of the alley, he heard the guard breaking more of the glass to get out. Ahead of him, the black SUV flew around the corner.

Jim stopped in his tracks as the truck barreled toward him. He ran at it, and tried to jump around the edge of the library and in to the parking lot.

The SUV hit his foot, and he went spinning head over heels. He landed with a loud thump on the asphalt. The world burned a bright white, and then faded to black.

Chapter 5

Jim slowly opened his eyes and looked around. He was in a cage. The designer of the cage had made it so it fit perfectly in to the back of the black SUV. It was late at night, and he could tell they were driving through the woods.

Occasionally a cabin with lights would flicker past, and then it was dark for half an hour. Jim felt tired, but was determined to stay awake.

After what felt like a day of endless driving through the dark, the SUV swerved on to a dirt road. Jim bounced in his cage. A tinted window slid open.

"You awake back there?" the man who had chased him asked.

"Yeah, what's it to you?" Jim said.

"Just wanted to make sure you were well enough to see the Boss," the guard said, sliding the window shut.

"Wait!" Jim shouted. The window slid back open.

"What?"

"Why'd you bring me here?"

"The computer code. Jeez, what a dimwit," the guard said, closing the window.

After an hour more, the SUV pulled up to a large three-story cabin. The guard opened the back doors to the truck and opened the cage door.

"Get out, kid, and don't run away."

Jim had no intention on running away. He had fallen deep in the pit, and was determined not to give up until he understood.

"Who are you?" Jim asked. "I thought the government caught all of Mr. Vaughn's spies."

"Yes, Hector Vaughn's spies, and guards have all been captured," the guard said, leading him in the side door to the cabin. "We work for someone else.

The guard led Jim down a quiet, dark hallway to a large metal door. The guard opened it and threw Jim in. Jim tumbled and landed on his back.

The door slammed closed, and he heard it lock. Above him, he saw a large dark shape lean over him. It was Sara Young.

"Jim, are you okay?"

"Yeah, but now my head hurts. How'd they get you?"

"They got me when I opened the door to my house. Didn't see them coming," Sara said, sitting down on the floor next to Jim. "How'd they get you?"

"They could only stop me by hitting me with their truck," Jim said, and they both laughed. It was odd, that for one moment Jim forgot where he was, and just laughed.

"Do you know why they brought us here?" Sara asked, bringing him back to reality.

"The guy who brought me here just kept babbling about some code," Jim said. "I couldn't figure out what he was talking about."

"Oh my gawd, the code?" Sara said.

"Wait, you know about this code?"

"Yeah, it's some code Greg wrote... I mean, *He* wrote to control realistic bomb detonation in a computer game."

The barrier of Greg was still between them. Jim thought something might have happened to him, but Sara thought he'd just forgotten them.

"So, this code, does it work in real life?" Jim asked.

"Yeah, it works so well that these guys apparently want it to make their own bombs."

"How does it work?"

"The bomb code is virtually unstoppable unless a certain code and radiation dose is used to deactivate it," Sara said.

"Do you know what it is?"

"No clue, only Greg knows for sure. He wrote the code, and must have hidden a copy at one of our houses."

"That's why they were after us, they think we have the code," Jim said.

"Genius," a voice came out of nowhere. "It is true; one of you has the code with you right now."

"Who is that?" Jim yelled at the walls.

"I am your host for this evening. I am sending one of our representatives to retrieve the code from you."

There was a long pause as dozens of thoughts ran through Jim's mind. Then the voice spoke again.

"Then I will have to interrogate you to see how much the Feds have learned. Afterwards, you'll be disposed of."

"What?" Sara yelled, hitting the walls, but the voice didn't answer. After several minutes of dead silence, the door swung open slowly. The light behind them silhouetted the person who stood in the door.

"Give me the code," the person said, and then stepped in to the dim light of the room.

It was Greg.

Chapter 6

"Greg, what do you think you're doing?" Sara yelled.

"Sorry, I have to. My... I have to," Greg said, staring at the ground. He walked over to Jim and grabbed his backpack.

He unzipped the front pocket and tore open a hole. Inside was a floppy disk. He took it and put it in his pocket. He turned and looked at Jim.

"I'm sorry, you don't understand."

"How can I understand?" Jim yelled. "You betray your best friends for some crazy spy?"

"You don't understand!" Greg yelled at him.

"No, no. I understand," Jim said. He slugged Greg in the stomach. "And that's my thoughts on it."

Greg stood up and quickly backed out of the room.

"Are you alright," Sara asked.

"Just get away," Jim said, pushing her away.

"Why'd you do that to Greg?" Sara said, coming back at him.

"I had to, don't you understand?"

"What, what's there to understand?"

"He's wrong, I'm right."

Sara looked bewildered.

"Come on, Sara. Ever since the first night we, broke in to Ms. Harcourt's office, he's just been a burden."

"No, he's helped in many ways," Sara said, pushing Jim. "You're just too thick to notice what anyone but you does."

"Me?!? Me!?!"

"Yeah, you."

"I could care less about what you think..."

Jim slammed his whole body against the door. *Slam!*

"What Greg thinks..."

He slammed in to it again. *Slam!*

"You will never..."

Slam!

"Never!"

Slam!

"NEVER!"

Slam!

"UNDERSTAND!"

SLAM!!! The door fell on to the hall floor. Jim collapsed in to a heap.

"Jim are you okay?"

"Just get away. GET AWAY!!!" Jim shoved her towards the wall. Sara hit it hard, and fell on to the floor. Jim looked up in surprise.

"Sara, are you okay?"

There was no response. Sara lay dead still.

"Sara?"

Jim's voice was higher, more scared.

"Sara? Sara?"

Jim crawled over to her and flipped her over. Blood trickled down the side of her face from the gash in her forehead.

"Sara, no! Sara, wake up!"

But Sara didn't move. The realization of what happened hit Jim. He was deep in the forest, surrounded by evil spies. One friend had betrayed him. And one friend was dead.

Chapter 7

"Jim, Jim!"

Jim turned around to see a familiar face running down the hallway toward him. It was Mr. Thompson.

"Jim, come quickly," Mr. Thompson said, then stopped.

"Sara." Jim could utter no more.

"I'll take her on my motorcycle," Mr. Thompson said. "I might be able to get medical attention."

Mr. Thompson's words sounded hopeful, but his face displayed the truth.

"Don't worry, I know how you feel. I lost a partner once in the field. Sandra was so nice and intelligent. I won't lose Sara too."

"Ok"

Jim sat back in the cell and watched Mr. Thompson run away with Sara slung over his shoulder. She was dead because of him.

All because he was obsessed with being right and investigating the stupid cameras. No one else was to blame.

He was the reason why Greg was working for a corrupt band of spies, Sara was dead, and Mr. Thompson was risking his life.

Jim couldn't take any more, and curled up in a ball on the floor. He fell asleep and for three hours, he was able to escape reality.

Nevertheless, as always happens, he was jerked back to reality by a sharp kick in the back.

He looked up to see someone looking down at him.

"Get up and tell us where your friend is."

Jim quickly stood up and looked at the man. He had a camouflage jacket and pants on. Jim thought he looked familiar.

"Where's your friend?"

"I don't know, she must have figured a way out while I was asleep." Jim tried to look as innocent as he could.

"Kyle, get a search party to look through the woods."

A man standing behind him saluted and ran down the hall.

"Come with me, kid."

He grabbed Jim by the back of the neck, and dragged him down the hall. They walked through miles of dark passageways until they finally came to a pure white room the size of a bedroom.

The man pointed to a hard wood chair.

"Sit."

Jim sat down. His mind was racing through all the things that could be happening. The man stood there for a minute, then turned and walked out.

After forever of waiting, the door slid open.

"I would like to introduce you to someone," the man said, walking in again. A dark and sinister man walked in after him.

"Mejev"

Chapter 8

The man sat down in a chair across the table and stared at Jim for what seemed like an hour. Jim began to worry slightly, but kept his cool.

"Why?" the man asked suddenly.

"Why, what?" Jim asked, caught off guard.

"Why'd you have to sneak in to your school that one night?"

Jim looked at him oddly. Mejev continued.

"I had something I wanted, I needed, to show my superior, but you ruined it. You had to interfere."

"Who are you? I thought Thompson caught all the spies working for Mr. Vaughn."

"Well, your dear friend Thompson missed me."

"So," Jim said, "you're just here to continue Mr. Vaughn's work?"

"Heck no," Mejev said. "His plans were awful. No organization, no motivation, *no drive*. I have much better plans than he did."

"Meh-jeh-v" Jim was talking to him self.

"What's that?" Mejev asked.

"Just thinking about names," Jim said. "Like, why is Sara's last name Young?"

"Huh?"

"Yeah, and why is Greg's Fields and why..."

Jim stopped. Every piece of the puzzle was beginning to fall in to place. Some people names were just consonants sounded out.

"Your name is Mejev!" Jim shouted. "It's your initials, MJV"

Mejev was silent.

"M for Matthew, your that guard from the hovercraft. J is for James or something like that. V for...," Jim paused, his eyes getting bigger. "V for Vaughn!"

"That's right, my father was Hector Vaughn!" Matthew suddenly yelled. "And you stupid kids killed him."

"No, he killed himself."

"No, he was a good man, a good man; you killed him when you stole his bomb."

Jim was paying attention, his mind was racing for the first time, and everything made sense. He realized who the man was who had led him in there.

"Your head spy," Jim said, "he's Hunter Fields, Greg's dad. That's why Greg couldn't help it."

"Yeah, he is."

"And he's the one who Sara said killed her mother. Her mom's name was, Sandra. I remember that name from somewhere else, too."

Matthew smiled. "I know her, she was annoying."

"Annoying? How could you know her?"

"We've met before. Sandra was nice."

Wait, Sandra was the name of Thompson's partner!"

"Ahh, idiot Thompson."

"That means Hunter's the one who killed Sara's mom, San…" Jim paused.

"Sandra, Sandra was Mr. Thompson's partner! She was killed trying to stop you!"

Matthew just smiled across the table.

Chapter 9

The door behind Matthew swung open; Greg flew in to the room. He swung the barrel of a shotgun down on Matthew's head, and Matthew fell to the floor.

"Jim, come on, let's get out of here," Greg said, pulling him up out of the chair.

Greg's father, Hunter, came flying around the corner.

"Matthew, what's wrong in there?" he shouted, and then saw Matthew, trying to stand up.

Jim and Greg ran through a door on the side wall of the room and found themselves in yet another dark corridor. Jim trailed close behind Greg, who seemed to know a little about where he was going.

Inherent Legacy

"This is my room," Greg said, opening the door.

The room was all white, with two single beds on opposite sides, and a chest of drawers on the wall the beds faced. Also on that wall was the door they had come through.

Directly across the room was a window. Jim ran over and looked out, but the window led to an inside courtyard. Jim stopped.

"How are we going to get out?"

"Simple," Greg said, grabbing his backpack off his bed. "Through the door to the right is the main control center. I... We need to do something there first, and then we can get out of the window in there."

Jim shoved the window open, and felt a blast of warm heat. He hadn't noticed how cool the inside of the building was. Jim started to climb out when there was a knock on the door.

"Not again," Jim said.

Chapter 10

Jim let go of the window ledge and dropped ten feet in to the flowerbeds below. Above, he heard Greg open the door.

"Hello, Nick."

"Hi, Greg. Your dad's lookin' for you, furious about something," Nick said. "What'd you do this time?"

"Stole his, um, motorcycle keys."

"Again?"

"Well, I... You know..."

"Come on, Greg. You've got to think of something new."

"Well, I better get out of here," Greg said. Jim saw him appear in the window above. "Bye, Nick. Oh, um, if I were you, I'd get out of here quickly."

Greg dropped down next to Jim.

"Come, on," Jim whispered. "I want to get out of here."

They snuck behind the tall plants, keeping low to the ground. Just before they got to the door, it swung open and a single guard ran out.

Greg went ahead of Jim and slowly opened the door and peeked in. Greg turned back to Jim and gestured.

"It's safe," Greg mouthed to Jim.

Jim still kept himself low to the ground and snuck over to the door. He also peeked in to the control center, but it was empty. Jim quickly ran in, and ran over to the door on the other side of the room.

Quickly, Jim and Greg locked all four doors leading to the room. Greg sat down at the main computer console, and began to type weird code in.

Jim noticed the vent leading in to the room, and reminded himself to watch so no one could sneak in that way. Greg reached under the desk and extracted a device.

In bright yellow on the top, it had the radiation hazard sign. Greg typed a few numbers in to it and set it on the desk. He also took out a dark metal cube.

"What is that?" Jim asked.

"It's the device used to deactivate the bomb," Greg said, fiddling with the miniscule control knobs. "It only works with the correct code and correct dose of radiation."

"That's almost fool-proof, depending on how the code and radiation dose are computed."

"I designed it for a video game mod. I had no idea that one day I would face it in real life."

Greg made one last adjustment. He stood back and admired his work. The dark metal deactivator, Greg's code cracker, and radiation modulator were all connected in a tangle of wires.

"Come on," Greg said. "We better get out of here before it's too late."

Greg opened the window and stuck one foot out. Jim walked over to the window, and then realized he had forgotten his backpack. He ran back to get it.

On his way back to the window, he tripped. He looked down at his foot and saw Hunter! Jim kicked hard, and Hunter let go.

"Get off, how'd you get in here?"

Jim answered his own question when he saw Hunter's feet still in the vent. He had forgotten about watching the vent. He kicked Hunter again and sprinted toward the window.

"Greg! Greg!"

Greg was halfway out, and turned back.

"What? Dad!"

Hunter barreled across the control room toward Jim and Jim rolled sideways. Hunter couldn't stop, though, and ran smack in to his son. Greg flew away from the second-story window and fell to the grass below.

"Greg, no!" Jim shouted, getting up and running toward the window. Hunter stood up and stopped his rush.

"Too late for you!"

Hunter's fist came down, and Jim barely made it out of the way. It smashed hard in to a control panel and the room began to flash red. An alarm was ringing and Jim's ears vibrated from the noise.

"Self-destruct in ten minutes."

Jim glanced around, looking for the abort button. He found it, but unfortunately, it was on the control panel Hunter had smashed.

Jim felt Hunter pick him up around the waist and hoist him high in the air. Jim could hardly breathe and felt like he was going to die any moment.

"So long, kid," Hunter said, throwing Jim out the window.

Chapter 11

Jim felt the air rush past him as he fell through the air. He saw something dark and large fly at him, and he grabbed at it. He flipped over the tree branch, but was able to hang on.

Every two seconds a short alarm sounded. In between, he thought he heard something below him. He dropped through the branches and found Greg lying on his back beneath the tree.

"Greg, are you okay?" Jim asked.

"No, I fell out of a second story window and tumbled down a thirty-foot hill."

A far-off buzzing sound appeared, and began to get closer. Jim looked up. It sounded almost identical to a helicopter. And a helicopter would have guns.

Jim carefully dragged Greg under a bush. The buzz was still a ways away, but was coming closer.

"Greg, are you okay?" Jim asked.

"Yeah, but my neck really, oww, hurts."

"Greg, don't die."

"What?"

"Sara, well, we were arguing and I accidentally pushed her too hard against the wall. I... I don't know if she'll be alright."

Greg began to sit up, using the tree for back support. The buzzing seemed to be dissipating.

"With all this life and death situation, it makes our arguing seem pointless, doesn't it?" Greg asked.

"Yeah, it does." Jim still stared at the ground.

"How about we promise that, if we live through this, we won't argue any more."

Jim looked up at him.

"At least," Greg continued, "we'll try very hard not to."

Jim looked back at the ground again, and then looked up.

"Deal."

He put out his hand. Greg offered his hand too, affirming the deal.

"For Sara."

"For Sara," Greg repeated.

The buzzing that had seemed to disappear for the last few minutes came back, louder than before.

Jim listened more carefully this time, and realized that the sound was coming from some sort of land vehicle.

"Greg, stay here," Jim said, standing up. "I have to see what's going on.

"Jim, wait," Greg pleaded, but Jim didn't listen.

He gazed around a large oak, and saw a headlight down a dirt path. The vehicle wasn't more than a hundred feet away, yet it sounded farther away.

Jim was trying to recognize the rider, when the vehicle turned toward him. He covered his eyes and cried in pain. The rider heard him, and revved the motorcycle.

Jim heard it, the motorcycle, flying down the path toward him, but couldn't bear to look. The motorcycle turned at the last second and skidded just three feet from Jim.

Opening his eyes, he saw a man wearing a dark green helmet with a black visor. Behind the visor was Mr. Thompson.

Chapter 12

"Thompson, how's Sara?" Jim asked.

"I don't know, the doctor wouldn't let me in to the med tent. Come on, let's get out of here."

"Wait, what about Greg?"

"Greg? The traitor?"

"He's not a traitor, he was just confused. He helped me escape."

Jim helped Greg stand up and walk over to the bike.

"Why do I always have to get hurt?" Greg asked. He looked at Jim. "Why can't you?"

A light beeping and buzz came from Greg's pocket. He quickly pulled out the small device. It was obviously a palm pocket Greg had added his own 'creativity' to.

"What is it?" Jim asked worriedly.

"The deactivator, it's been disabled. I have to set it back up."

"Six minutes to control room self destruct."

The computerized voice echoed through the building and surrounding woods. Greg glanced down at his controller. He frowned.

"They have a bomb set already," he said. "It goes off ten seconds before the self-destruct."

"Where is it?" Thompson asked, pulling out his walkie-talkie.

"Calculating coordinates. There are three, all activated by the same device."

"Where are they?" Thompson asked again.

Greg typed some more in to his device.

"They are all in the IDS building, downtown Minneapolis."

"Five minutes, thirty seconds, to control room self-destruct."

"Jim, I will go and see if we can set it back up," Thompson said, running up the hill and trying to climb up the wall. He was having a hard time, though, because it was smooth concrete, with no cracks.

"Thompson, the only way in is through the vents," Greg said.

"Hurry then, help me find one."

Jim and Greg ran all around the wall, but couldn't find a ventilation shaft. Finally, Greg spotted one.

"Jim, Thompson, come quickly."

Jim ran around the corner to see Greg looking up. Jim also looked up and saw what he saw. Ten feet up the wall, the wood paneling started, and at the edge was a vent.

"Someone has to be lifted up," Thompson said, running up.

"Greg, me and Thompson will hoist you up so you can reactivate the deactivator."

"No, I can't crawl with my leg. It's too weak."

"Jim, you'll have to go," Thompson said, grabbing his foot.

Jim grabbed at the concrete to help steady himself, but he couldn't pull himself up. Mr. Thompson pushed a little higher, and Jim was able to grab the edge of the vent and pull himself in.

Aaron Achartz

As he began to crawl through the vent, he heard the loudspeaker outside announce, "Four minutes to control room self-destruct."

Chapter 13

The dust filled the air as Jim half crawled, half-slid down the vent at top speed. He took a quick right at the first fork, and found himself at a dead end.

He tried to back up, but it took him a while. He wasted precious seconds getting out and continued on his way even quicker. The voice once again echoed through the vents.

"Three minutes to control room self-destruct."

Jim turned right at the next intersection and after twenty feet, found himself at another fork. He felt he had gone too far in to the building, and turned right to head back toward the outer wall.

The ventilation shaft ended in a quick left turn and the grate. Jim looked out and realized that Hunter had come in the vent on the opposite side of the room.

Pushing hard against the grate, Jim was able to get in to the room. He jumped up, and didn't even bother to wipe the dust off himself. He ran over to the table and turned on his walkie-talkie.

"Greg, Greg?" Are you there?"

"I'm here, are you in?"

"Yeah, I'm looking at it right now. All that's left is the radiation device and the metal box. Your decoder's gone."

"You'll have to solve the code yourself," Greg said.

"How?" Jim asked, almost dropping the walkie-talkie.

"Well, first you take the number it displays on the screen and..."

"Two minutes until control room self-destruct"

"Take the number," Greg continued, "and multiply it by three. Then divide by two and cube it. Find the square root, and..."

Jim was furiously typing the information in to the calculator. He slipped and pushed the wrong button.

"Wait, wait Greg. Say it over again, I made a mistake," Jim said, this time dropping the walkie-talkie.

Greg quickly repeated the instructions.

"Take the number, multiply it by fo... no, three. Multiply the number by three. Divide it by two and cube it. Next, find the square root of that. Finally, multiply by ten and round to the nearest whole number," Greg finished up.

"Okay, 41.56. That must round up to 42."

Jim quickly typed in forty-two in to the metal box, but it beeped at him.

"Greg, it's not working," Jim said, grabbing the walkie-talkie off the floor.

"One minute to control room self-destruct."

"It has to work, I... Wait, Jim you have to set the radiation modulator up correctly."

"How?" Jim yelled in to the walkie-talkie. He was starting to sweat, the room seemed hotter.

Greg's heavy breathing was amplified by the walkie-talkie's microphone. Greg didn't answer.

"Greg, come on. I only have thirty seconds."

The airwaves were still silent. Then, Greg spoke.

"I don't remember."

Chapter 14

"Greg, come on, Minneapolis, no, *the world* is counting on us!"

"I can't remember how to solve it, but there was a certain dosage of radiation that always works."

Jim set the radiation modulator up and against the deactivator. All he needed was to enter the code, and get out of there.

"Greg, come on."

"Forty-five seconds to control room self-destruct."

Jim had only thirty-five seconds to enter the radiation dosage. The door leading to the courtyard swung open and Hunter came barreling in to the room.

"You! Get away from there!"

Jim jumped out of the way. As Hunter ran by, he threw him on to the ground. Hunter quickly jumped to his feet.

"Leave it alone kid, you don't know what you're messing with."

"Thirty seconds to control room self-destruct."

Jim heard a motorcycle fly out of the woods, and he looked out the window. On the motorcycle was Sara.

Sara was alive! She must have gotten better and come to help. But if she didn't know the number to enter, they were doomed.

"Jim, Sara's here!" Greg shouted through the radio. "The number is..."

Hunter smashed his fist on to the radio.

"We'll all die now, kid," he said, smirking.

"Twenty seconds to control room self-destruct."

Jim had only ten seconds to get the number. But what would it be? What number would Greg always remember?

"Your son is the one who's going to save the world, by debunking his code!"

"My son is a loser!"

"No, he isn't!"

"Fifteen seconds to control room self-destruct."

"He always thinks he's number one!"

One! It hit Jim like a punch in the stomach.

He ran and slid under Hunter. He grabbed the radiation modulator and typed in one. He aimed it at the deactivator.

The deactivator beeped. And shut off.

"Ten seconds to control room self-destruct."

Jim had ten seconds to leave, or he would be barbequed. He hadn't even thought about stopping the control room self-destruct sequence.

Hunter stood sneering at Jim. Then the realization that he was in the control room hit him. He raced across the room towards the door to the courtyard.

Jim ran across the other way. He tried to sidestep Hunter, but the bull of a man hit him and he fell to the floor.

"Five seconds to control room self-destruct."

Jim tried to stand up and tripped over his feet. Standing up quickly again, he grabbed on to the window ledge and threw himself out the window.

As he flew through the air, the control room exploded behind him in a massive fireball.

Chapter 15

Jim flew through the air for the second time in ten minutes. Once again, he reached for the tree branch, but he didn't see it. He fell down, and landed on something soft.

It was Greg.

"Jim, are you okay?" Sara asked, running up to him.

"Yeah, I'm fine, and are you okay?"

"Yeah, I'm fine."

"I'm sorry Sara."

"It's okay... Jeez, I'm glad to be done with this," Sara said, changing the subject. "Did you find all the guys working here?"

Thompson shook his head.

"No, Hunter and two other guards we couldn't find in the woods surrounding here. I figured they must have stayed in the building."

When he mentioned the cabin, Jim turned to look back at it. A huge fireball lit the night sky and all that was left of the cabin was a torched outline.

"Greg, sorry but I left your walkie-talkie thing in the control room."

Greg just laughed. "I guess it's *well-done* now."

All four of them laughed. Jim felt great now that all the tension was gone. He felt like he was on top of the world, despite how much his arm hurt.

Thompson's radio crackled.

"Thompson, are you there?" the voice on the radio asked.

"Yes, I'm here. What is it?"

"We caught the last two guards that we could not find in the woods I think Hunter's dead. I'm holding the guards in custody on the north side of the cabin."

"I'll be right over." Thompson turned off his radio.

"Well, we got everyone," Sara said.

"I'm never doing this spy stuff again," Jim said. They all laughed.

Aaron Achartz

The End

About the Author

Aaron Achartz is a sophomore at Hopkins High School. He lives in Minnetonka, Minnesota with three females. He lives with his mother, Julie Mohlis, his sister, Sarah Achartz, and a one-year-old American Eskimo dog, Lexi.

Aaron's hobbies include reading and creating comics on the computer. In addition to these, he enjoys taking long walks with his dog, Lexi to "just think". His favorite hobby, by far, is writing. This is Aaron's first published book.